Thanks for reading!

Stay pink,

[signature]

Pink HAIR and Other TERRIBLE Ideas

by Andrea Pyros

CAPSTONE EDITIONS
a capstone imprint

Pink Hair and Other Terrible Ideas is published by Capstone Editions
1710 Roe Crest Drive
North Mankato, Minnesota 56003
www.mycapstone.com

Library of Congress Cataloging-in-Publication Data
Names: Pyros, Andrea, author.
Title: Pink hair and other terrible ideas / by Andrea Pyros.
Description: North Mankato, Minnesota : Capstone Editions, [2019] | Summary: When seventh grader Josephine's mother is diagnosed with breast cancer, she wants to keep it secret, even from her best friend, Makayla, but her twin brother, Chance, has other ideas.
Identifiers: LCCN 2018029008 (print) | LCCN 2018035123 (ebook) | ISBN 9781684460298 (eBook PDF) | ISBN 9781684460281 (hardcover)
Subjects: | CYAC: Middle schools—Fiction. | Schools—Fiction. | Breast—Cancer—Fiction. | Cancer—Fiction. | Brothers and sisters—Fiction. | Twins—Fiction. | Single-parent families—Fiction.
Classification: LCC PZ7.1.P975 (ebook) | LCC PZ7.1.P975 Pin 2019 (print) | DDC [Fic]—dc23
LC record available at https://lccn.loc.gov/2018029008

Designer: Kay Fraser
Design elements on cover courtesy of Shutterstock

Printed and bound in China.
001764

Dedicated to Marc and Beth,
still the coolest twins ever.
And to Kate, Amy, and Marvin. Thank you.

1

The day I realized I was an awful human being began like any other seventh-grade school day.

Days that go down the toilet always start off completely fine and normal. They only get screwy *after* you think dribbling toothpaste down the front of your favorite sweater will be the worst thing to happen. (In the battle between clean laundry and toothpaste, toothpaste always wins.)

Like a regular Tuesday, remembering to bring my oboe for my music class?

Check.

Tacos for Taco Tuesday in the cafeteria?

Yep.

Hiding near the wall at the back of the gym, pretending to "hustle" during floor hockey while Ms. Edells, my P.E. teacher, shouted commands?

You know it.

After-school chess club with my best friend, Makayla?

Both of us present and accounted for.

It's 3:07, and Makayla and I are right where we always are on Tuesday afternoon, sitting in the cluttered art room of Westchester North Middle School with the other seven members of our school's chess team.

"*J'adoube!*" Makayla says, using the term that allows her to adjust a piece so it's centered perfectly in the middle of its square.

I giggle. "Makayla, it's just me. If you want to futz around with your bishop so it's lined up, you don't have to call it."

She rolls her eyes at me. "I know, I'm just practicing. I wouldn't want to get disqualified during an actual tournament for wanting my pieces to look neat."

Last year, Makayla read an issue of *Us Weekly* that listed ten stars who have obsessive-compulsive disorder. They tap out "Heart and Soul" nonstop on the steering wheel as they're driving, or have to knock eight times before opening a door, or can't handle it if one pencil in their cup holder is shorter than all the others.

For a while Makayla thought she might have OCD too, but I convinced her that wanting things to be neat wasn't the same as having a real disease. Now she says she has "a love of order."

And really, if Makayla wants to line up her pieces perfectly in the center of her squares, I'm not going to complain. I was the one who roped her into joining chess club with me last year at the start of sixth grade, our first year in middle school. Sadly I'm not all that accomplished at most things . . . like I don't have some awesome talent for holding my breath underwater or skateboarding. But before my parents divorced, I played chess with my dad on nights he didn't have a gig, so I was psyched to join an after-school activity where I was basically guaranteed not to be the worst. Plus there wasn't any team or other club I was dying to join, and doing nothing at all felt pathetic.

Makayla has been a good sport about coming along with me to chess, even though I was too chicken to sign up for the cheer/dance team with her in return. I can't do splits to save my life, and I once got a painful scratch on my eye from a pom-pom string the year we dressed as cheerleaders for Halloween. Plus standing up in front of a bajillion gawking faces is my absolute worst nightmare. Makayla might get some butterflies in her stomach, but she likes that feeling! Having a bold friend is good, I tell myself. It motivates you to do stuff.

"Josephine, I'm calling it right now. Autumn's party will be *the* party of the year!" Makayla whispers as she takes one of my rooks.

It's a downright impressive move, especially considering she isn't even fully concentrating on the game. She's too busy obsessing about our classmate Autumn's upcoming birthday party. Autumn is one of the most popular girls at school and the first in our grade to turn thirteen, so her party is a big deal. Although even if Autumn weren't popular, Makayla would be psyched about it. She loves a party.

"It's September," I say. "The school year is a few weeks in. You can't already declare this is the party of the year."

Makayla grins. "I know a good party when I hear about it."

"So when is it?" I ask, copying Makayla's whisper.

She shrugs. "All I know is what Emily told me before the bell rang. That Autumn decided she's having a thirteenth birthday party after all. Emily isn't sure who's invited or when it's happening."

Emily is Autumn's best friend, and Makayla does cheer with both of them. Ever since they all went to a sleepaway camp over the summer, Makayla and I have been sitting at their table during lunch.

"I'm sure you're invited, Makayla. You spent an entire week with them at cheer camp," I tell her. I, on the other hand, am currently at the friends-with-Autumn-because-we're-both-friends-with-Makayla stage, so whether I get to go is a different story.

I study the chessboard, feeling stuck on what to do next. Makayla's a better chess player than I am, even though I started playing years before her. She's already better than most of the eighth graders in our chess club too. She credits it all to her "love of order." But really it's because her genius is hidden. People underestimate her because she wears shirts that say: CHEER LOUD, CHEER PROUD or IT'S HARD TO BE HUMBLE WHEN YOU CAN JUMP,

STUNT, AND TUMBLE!, and on game days she applies hair chalk in streaks that match her uniform. They assume she's not serious and then, *BAM! Checkmate, fool!*

That's a good life lesson for everything, not just in chess: Never underestimate anyone! Admittedly it can be annoying that Makayla is so good at chess, because she's good at *everything*, but playing against her has made me better. That part is awesome. Now when Dad and I play— not that we do that much anymore—I usually win more often than not.

"Autumn *always* has the party of the year," Makayla continues, waiting for me to make my move. "Always, always, *always*. Remember the year she rented out Splash-World for the whole grade? Or the party where her parents had limos take everyone to the drive-in for a movie? Or the time the Olympic gymnast came to her family's private gym to teach us how to use the uneven bars, and we got warm-up suits as the party favor? With our names stitched on the front?"

As she speaks, Makayla takes one of the Day-Glo green hair bands on her wrist and pulls her curly, dark brown hair off her face. It's finally at the perfect length, grown out from the disastrous, poufy haircut she got at Tress for Less, the hair salon in our little town of Croton-on-Hudson, New York. After that debacle Makayla insisted she'd be sticking with Black Hair Is, the salon forty-five minutes away in New York City that her mom goes to. At least until someone who can figure out how to cut a black girl's hair without butchering it moves to our town.

I don't have to worry about trips to the city for fancy salons. My hair is easy to cut because it's, as Makayla calls it, "white girl straight." I keep it one length and almost always pulled back in clips or hair ties. Mom usually trims it in our bathroom.

I nod at Makayla, still studying the board until I finally make a move with my knight. Of course I remember all Autumn's awe-inspiring parties. It would be too easy to be teeth-gnashingly envious of her. Who wouldn't be jealous of someone who rented out *an entire water park* before it opened to the public? But the thing is, Autumn is actually nice. Yes, she's so rich it's like pretend-movie-star-rich instead of real-life rich, and yes, she can be over the top about it, but she has a good heart, and she's generous with others. Although maybe it's easy to be generous when a warm-up hoodie is to her family what a single stick of gum is to mine. Regular old Trident, I mean. Not the fancy brand with the squirty center.

Just then Mrs. Fletcher, the eighth-grade history teacher and our chess coach, comes by. "Ms. Doukas." She nods to me. "Ms. Kaiser," she says to Makayla. "Next time, pick one of our new sixth-grade members to partner with. Let them get some practice with you old hands."

"OK," Makayla replies with a smile. As soon as Mrs. Fletcher walks away, she leans back over the board and continues dishing details. "Emily says this year Autumn wants a small, low-key party. That's why she almost didn't have one in the first place; she didn't want to make a big deal out of it. But since there are only going to be a few people invited, it'll probably still be major. Like a fancy dinner party at a cool restaurant. Or maybe she'll get people picked up in limos or send them home with their own Vespas or something. We totally have to go! If we don't, we'll be hearing stories about it until we graduate!"

I understand what Makayla means. Low-key for Autumn is still a big deal. And getting an invite *does* sound amazing, but I don't want to obsess about it. I made a back-to-school promise to myself to keep my focus on what really matters: my grades. I got a taste of being on the honor roll during sixth grade, and I really liked how it felt to have that certificate mailed to me at the end of the quarter. This year I want to make that happen all four quarters instead of just one, which means I can't waste all my energy wishing for a party invitation.

"I'm sure Chance could get us invited," Makayla says, looking hopeful. "Like, you know, work his Chance magic."

I resist the urge to roll my eyes. My twin could not care less who likes him or doesn't, so of course that means everyone worships him. A lot of girls at our school have crushes on him and not-so-subtly ask me if he's dating anyone—*no*—and how come I don't have green eyes or white-blond hair like him—*how should I know?* My hair is regular old brown. My eyes are regular old brownish green. I have one eye that closes a bit more when I smile. That's the extent of my edgy beauty.

Makayla once asked me if it made me jealous that Chance was basically the king of our middle school, but I'm not.

"Is a horse jealous of a unicorn?" I said, trying to explain myself to her.

Even though she's my best friend and knows me so well, Makayla didn't get it. "Uh, hello, yes!" she answered. "Is this a trick question?"

But it wasn't. It's more like Chance is a clueless, speckled, goofy unicorn who's always knocking stuff over with his horn and can't manage to stand still and eat his hay like the rest of us. I'm not jealous of him. Being that hyper all the time and always being noticed for just being *himself* seems exhausting.

I'm way happier blending in.

Most of the time.

I thought it was easier that way. But it turns out awful things can happen whether you stand out or not.

2

On chess club days, Makayla's mom, Mrs. Kaiser, picks us both up from school and drops me off at my house on their way home. My mom normally gets home around five o'clock from her job as assistant manager of an office supply store. It's not exactly the world's most exciting job, but we do have a lot of free sample pens and paper in our house. One year Mom gave out orange, foot-long pencils on Halloween to the trick-or-treaters, but that didn't go over so well. Now we do Smarties like everyone else and our porch gets to stay shaving cream and toilet paper free.

I let myself into the house that afternoon, waving goodbye to Makayla as she yells out the car window, "I'll text you the second I hear anything about Autumn's party!"

I should immediately turn on the computer to start working on my history essay, "What Was the Spark That Started World War I?" which is due in three days, but I instead let Chance talk me into playing *Farming Simulator* with him. And even though I promised myself I wouldn't think about it, I keep glancing at my cell phone to see if Makayla has texted. So much for my resolution to focus on the important things.

I lie down on the carpet, my face close to the screen, while Chance sprawls out on the big striped easy chair, letting his long legs dangle over the armrest. In the past year Chance grew taller than me by about a half a foot, and now he's all knees and elbows and limbs, like how people draw stick figures. His hair grew out over the summer too, so shaggy blond strands keeps flicking into his eyes as we play. I don't understand how it doesn't bother him. I'm distracted by it, and it's not even my face.

During our attempt to grow more virtual potatoes, Mom gets home from work a full hour earlier than usual and comes into the living room where Chance and I are playing.

"Hi, Mom," I say to her as I watch my tractor on the screen, halfheartedly curious as to why she's home early—her hours are pretty firm at work.

"Hey," Chance says, waving over his shoulder, one of his long arms just inches from Mom's face.

Mom keeps standing there, staring at us. Then she takes a deep breath, loud enough to be heard over the noise of the game, and sits down in the middle of the couch. "Why don't you two turn that off?" she says, patting the cushions on each side of her.

Chance and I look at each other quizzically. When Mom gets home, she's usually all about checking the mail and getting into her red sweatpants and making dinner and bugging us to see if we've done our homework, which I usually have and Chance usually hasn't. She doesn't sit on the couch and talk about our days or the weather or whatever it is people who have free time on their hands talk about.

Even before Mom and Dad divorced, back when we were in third grade, Mom always seemed to be rushing around between work and making dinner and getting us places and running errands. Dad doesn't like to rush for anything, and he wasn't much on doing parental chores, even when he lived with us full time.

Chance and I flop down onto the couch on either side of her, and I take out my cell phone to make sure I haven't missed any important, breaking news alerts from Makayla. Nothing. I slide it back into my pocket just as Mom says, "So last week I had a few tests done."

Chance and I look at each other again. "What kind of tests?" I ask, not liking the way Mom's voice sounds unnaturally even, like she's recording a voicemail greeting.

She clasps her hands together. They're shaking slightly.

"I was in the shower a few weeks ago, and I felt something in my armpit under the skin. Like a hard pebble. I thought it was a bug bite, so I waited a few days, but when it didn't go away I went to see my doctor. And then he sent me to another doctor who did a test—an X-ray type of thing—and then a biopsy."

Chance looks puzzled, but I'm not confused. I'm *scared*. I know that Mom wouldn't be listing all these doctors' appointments if they weren't a big deal. Just the word *biopsy* is frightening.

I pray I'm wrong, that Mom is telling us a crazy story that will end with all of us cracking up, but the look on her face isn't one of a person about to bust out a punch line. I have to stop myself from flying out of the room as she takes another deep breath. Her mouth looks even sadder now, like an upside-down clown face.

"They sent it to a lab and today I met with a new doctor to talk about the results. It's cancer. Breast cancer."

A brick drops down into my stomach, settling there heavy and hard. "But you said under your arm," I say, "not in your . . ." I gesture to my front.

"It's confusing. They call it breast cancer even if it's in your armpit. I don't know why." Mom reaches out to squeeze our hands. Her hands feel dry, and the tips of her fingers are rough from all the paper cuts she gets at work. She's still wearing her name tag, which reads: Hi, I'm Allison. Ask me how to save on printer paper today. A button on her shirt has popped open, and I can see her beige bra underneath—nothing looks wrong with her body. She looks like regular Mom, down to the lipstick that's faded with the day.

"Isn't breast cancer serious?" Chance asks, biting down on his fingernail.

"Well . . . there are different stages of cancer. Mine may only be at stage two."

"Which is good, right?" I say. "If you're only stage two?"

Mom shakes her head and then pauses for a while before saying, "I don't have all the details, honey. But my doctor seemed very positive and upbeat."

"So he was upbeat like, 'Whoopee, you have cancer, let's have a parade!'?" I ask, near tears. *What kind of jerk doctor is upbeat about cancer? And why is Mom using words like* upbeat *and* cancer *in the same sentence?*

"It's a she, actually. Dr. Chernoff. She's a breast cancer specialist, so she knows what she's talking about, and she assures me this disease is very, *very* treatable."

Chance stays silent for a few minutes, but my brother isn't ever quiet for long. Without warning he bursts into tears. Not quiet tears either. The kind where your whole face gets wet right away, and the tears come leaping out of your eyes like they're running for their lives.

"Are you going to die?" he says, his face crumpling in on itself like a piece of paper being crushed into a ball. Even his body seems to shrink down. Suddenly he looks small and young, not like an almost-thirteen-year-old who's as tall as Mom.

There's a sound like water rushing in my ears, and my face feels hot. Chance always says what other people— usually, me—are thinking but don't want to say. And like always, it seems we're thinking the same thing at the same time. *What if something happens to her? What will happen to us without her?*

Mom doesn't respond at first. She just gives Chance a big hug. I don't look at her. I'm worried I'll scare her if she sees my face before I can get my features under control. One of us has to stay calm, especially if Chance is going to get all loud and sobby.

Just then my cell phone beeps loudly from the back pocket of my jeans, making all three of us jump. I turned the volume all the way up earlier so I'd be sure to hear any texts from Makayla over the noise of the video game.

I ignore it.

"Don't worry, honey," Mom says, squeezing Chance's shoulder one more time and then giving my stiff body a hug too. She smells nice, like the perfume she sometimes wears but usually forgets to spritz on because she's always rushing so much in the mornings. "Dr. Chernoff even said that if you have to have cancer, breast cancer is one of the best kinds to have."

She sounds almost cheerful, which I know has to be an act for us, because Mom isn't even cheerful about small stuff that goes wrong. Like last summer, when a chipmunk leaped out of our barbeque grill and scared her so much that she dropped a platter of corn on the ground. There was zero cheer then.

"Now what happens?" Chance asks. "Are you going to have chemotherapy?"

Mom looks surprised by Chance's question, like she didn't expect him to know what chemotherapy was.

"Not right away," she says. "First I'll have surgery where they'll go in and remove the tumor. After that the doctors will know more about our next steps, which might be radiation therapy and then medications I can take after to really kick the crap out of this cancer." Mom makes an unimpressive fist and pretends to punch something. Her bottom lip wobbles a tiny bit. "And I already called your father and filled him in. When I do have to go to the hospital, I'll stay there at least one night, so he'll come here to babysit you."

"Babysit?" Chance rolls his eyes. "We're in seventh grade! We haven't needed a babysitter since . . . forever!"

"You already told Dad?" I ask. "When?"

"I called him last week to tell him I was having the biopsy and then today once I knew more about what was going on."

"Wait. You told Dad before you told us?" I say. *"Dad?"*

"Yes, *Dad* as in your father, Richard Doukas. He's concerned about all of us, and he wants to be here while I'm in the hospital to make sure things run smoothly. Then when I get home, Aunt Nora will come stay for a few days."

Aunt Nora makes sense. She lives a few hours away, in a suburb of Philadelphia, but she and Mom talk all the time. She's actually Dad's sister, but she and Mom stayed close after the divorce. Mom doesn't have any siblings of her own.

Chance gives an angry snort through his dripping nose and tears. "Dad?! Come on."

Dad isn't really the "run smoothly" type. For starters, he's a trumpet player in a jazz ensemble. He's the guy who doesn't have to wake up before eleven. He's the man who gets divorced and then immediately starts dating a backup singer who's twenty years younger.

Don't get me wrong, Dad is nonstop fun. I love Dad. Everyone who meets Dad loves him. It's also impossible to stay angry at him. He shrugs his shoulders or cracks a joke and no matter how infuriating he can be, we all forgive him.

Except my brother.

Chance is still mad at Dad about the divorce. When our parents first separated, Mom got us a book for kids whose parents break up. It had little illustrations throughout it that were dumb, but the actual words were good. It started off with an entire chapter called, "It's Not Your Fault!"

I already knew that, but I think for a long time, Chance felt like the divorce *was* our fault. And once he started to realize it had nothing to do with us, he decided it was all Dad's fault.

I don't believe that, though. Some people just aren't meant to live together, and Dad and Mom are the definition of *incompatible*. It's not Dad's fault that Mom isn't as fun as he is, just like it's not Mom's fault that Dad isn't as responsible or grown up as she is.

While they were together, their strengths balanced each other out. Apart, it's easier to notice their flaws.

But coming to *help* while Mom is in the hospital? I am so with Chance on that; Dad won't even know where to begin. When we visit him, we get slices of pizza or McDonald's or Chinese food from a takeout place around the corner from his basement apartment in Philadelphia. He brings us to his gigs, and we stay up late drinking ginger ales at the back table while he and the band perform.

Does he even have a stove in his dinky apartment? I can't remember. He's never prepared anything more elaborate for us than a bowl of cereal for breakfast. Unlike with Mom, there won't be any Meatball Monday or Burrito Friday going on while Dad is here.

Mom wipes away a tear from her eyes and smiles. "Your father is perfectly capable. It's not like there will be all that much to handle. I'll be gone for a few nights at most, and you two are so on top of things." Her voice breaks. "I'm so proud of you both. You're such wonderful . . ."

Mom can't seem to finish her sentence. The silence is too awful to bear, so I ask what I haven't stopped imagining since the second she said the word *breast*. "Are they going to cut off your whole chest? Like . . . everything?" The words barely squeeze free from my tight throat.

Mom pauses for a minute, looking down and picking at the button on her shirt, before she faces me. "I'm not sure exactly what my plan is yet. My doctor told me that some women choose to remove just a small area where the cancer is located. Others opt for a different approach. A more full . . . removal. I don't know yet."

I think about that word. *Removal*. Does that mean cutting off an entire part of her body? Won't it hurt? It sounds painful and scary.

"But, Mom, maybe you won't need any surgery. Does everyone have to have do that?" Chance says.

"Try not to worry." Mom rubs her left eye with the heel of her hand, smudging some of her mascara onto her cheek. "I know it's easier said than done, but I don't want you to be scared. I'm going to be fine. We're *all* going to be OK."

I feel . . . something. A lot of things. A big jumbo mix of feelings all at once, but I'm not sure exactly what they are, besides terrified. Kind of like when Chance and I were eight and Mom and Dad told us about the divorce. It wasn't a complete surprise since Dad was gone so much at night and they fought all the time about "responsibility" and "being an adult." But this? This is beyond unexpected. It's beyond shocking. How could things go from regular and normal to the worst in an instant?

My heart is racing, and I feel sick to my stomach. I can't stop picturing Mom in a hospital, surrounded by doctors and tubes and wires and beeping machines. The visual is so realistic that it takes me a minute to realize the series of beeps is coming from my cell phone, not my imagination.

Mom laughs. "Josephine, that is incredibly loud. Please tell me you don't have it turned up like that at school."

"Mom, of course not!" I say, guilty about the interruption when she was talking about something so important, and even guiltier that during the worst moment of our lives, I still want to know what the messages say.

"Josephine, it's fine to answer it," Mom says, reading my mind. She gestures toward my pocket where my phone is peeking out. "Go about your normal business."

I pull my phone out. The texts are from Makayla and in all caps:

TALKED TO AUTUMN GUESS WHAT?

I'M INVITED TO HER PARTY! YESS!!!

AND GUESS WHO ELSE IS???

CMON THREE GUESSES!

TWO GUESSES?

ONE GUESS????

WELL SINCE YOURE NOT GUESSING ILL TELL YOU. YOU ARE!

HALLLOoooooooO??! WHERE ARE YOU?

Reading Makayla's texts gives me a tiny happy blip in a sea of feeling terrible. Which makes me wonder if I'm the most horrible daughter in the world. How can anything *so small* make me happy when something *so big* is so awful?

I take a deep breath. Our living room seems warm, and I'm spacey, like when you go to the movies on the hottest day of the summer and have to walk back across the parking lot to the car when it's over. Everything is shimmery and unreal, heat rising off the hot pavement, and it feels like it's already been hours since you were in a cool, air-conditioned space, not minutes.

"I'm going to my room," I say, standing up and accidentally knocking Mom's white canvas tote onto the floor. It lays there, sadly. The bag still has the bright purple scarf Chance and I gave her for Mother's Day wrapped around one of the handles as decoration.

The scarf was pretty when Chance and I argued over buying it for her—he wanted to get her earrings, but I insisted she'd use a scarf more. Maybe he was right, because I don't think she's ever worn it. Now it seems forlorn, all twisted and wrapped up, one end fraying, like it's been dragged along unwillingly from home to work and back again, never getting to do anything fun.

I swallow hard, blinking my eyes.

Mom smiles at me. A lot of the time when I want to be by myself she tries to get me to stay with everyone else. I think she worries about me feeling lonely. She's an only child, so it's hard for her to understand that it's impossible to find enough time to yourself to be lonely when you're half of a pair.

This time she watches me leave without saying a word.

I head to my room and gingerly climb into bed, feeling incredibly tired. Then my phone beeps again.

Where are u? Makayla texts. I can almost hear her voice—which would no doubt sound like squeals of joy.

here, I write back.

ahem did you not see my last message?

saw it

I doubt that bc otherwise the thank you flowers youd have ordered for me for getting us invited would have arrived already

i never doubted you

I know I should tell her. This is the exact right moment to tell my best friend that my mother has cancer. *Cancer!* It would be weird *not* saying something—my mind can't focus on anything else.

Except I don't.

I keep typing *Mom has . . .* or *I just found out that . . .* or *guess what* and then erasing my words, heart racing. Part of me is desperate for Makayla to know, but the thought of making it official makes my stomach hurt worse.

What if Mom's doctors are wrong and it's not even cancer? Or they caught it so early that she won't even need surgery or chemotherapy or anything, just some pills? Or maybe it will disappear the same way it magically appeared in the first place?

So I pretend everything is normal to Makayla.

Who else is coming?! I type.

Not sure! Definitely you, me, Autumn, Emily. I think Anna but don't say anything in case I'm wrong, k?

Anna is the other girl we usually sit with at lunch. She moved to Croton during the middle of sixth grade and is super outgoing, so she made friends with everyone right away.

k, I won't say anything! When is the party?

Autumn is still picking a date. Her mom has to be out of town to shoot a commercial so she's waiting to find out when she'll be back before she picks a date

Cool

I add a few smiley faces and a photo of a dog wearing sunglasses.

By the time we're done texting about the party, the moment for me to say anything about Mom has passed.

It's like climbing all the way up to the high dive and then deciding you're willing to climb all the way back down again instead of jumping. Once you decide not to do something at the very last second, working up your nerve the next time is almost impossible.

3

"I have to talk to you . . . NOW," Makayla says, grabbing my upper arm as I'm putting my books into my locker the next morning.

At first I think she's heard about my mom somehow, and my heart gives a hard thump in my chest. It reverberates all the way down to my fingertips.

"What's wrong?" I ask.

"Wrong? Nothing. Why would something be wrong?" Makayla giggles. "Did I seem dramatic there? I want to talk about the party."

"Oh, whew," I say, "I thought there was an emergency."

"Only my fashion emergency." Makayla looks down at her zigzag leggings and wrinkles up her face.

Makayla looks great, like always, but she aspires to a higher style calling than most people. Certainly higher than I do. Today I'm wearing my beloved yellow INTROVERTS UNITE! INDIVIDUALLY shirt.

Before she can say anything else, the bell rings.

"I have to go," I say, grabbing my notebook out of my backpack and shutting my locker door. Then I stop and reach over to give Makayla a hug, looking for comfort, even if she doesn't know why.

She gives me a funny look—unlike most people, I'm not a huge hugger—but squeezes me back. "Find me at lunch!" she yells.

As soon as she walks away I feel incredibly alone. Makayla is good at keeping my spirits up and making me forget things that are awful, like studying for tests or how I always get a pimple between my eyebrows when it's school picture time. She even helped me forget my disastrous crush on Ethan Gallagher. I liked him for almost all sixth grade and then—finally, miraculously!—he liked me back. That lasted an entire week, until I missed a kick during kickball, and our team lost the stupid "World Cup" tournament. Ethan told *everyone* in the whole school he didn't like me after all and made up a nickname for me: Jo Blows. Sigh.

To cheer me up, Makayla showed up at my house with supplies to make slime—clear and glitter—plus muffins she'd baked. It took a while for the nickname—and my crush—to fade, but Makayla's efforts at least helped distract me and made me feel less alone. She even got me to laugh by making up mean nicknames for Ethan.

That was the second worst day of my life, after the day my parents told us about the divorce.

That is, until last night.

* * *

I have math first period. During the summer I was moved into advanced math because I did so well in regular math class last year. It's always been my favorite subject. Everything always looks so neat and organized, and numbers behave in logical, understandable ways. This year we've even gotten into plotting cool charts and graphs.

But during class today I can't focus on the lecture at all. I keep looking up at the clock like I'm waiting for something to happen, even though the past twenty-four hours have been more than enough *something* for me. When Mrs. Grunwald asks me to explain mean, median, mode, and range, I get flustered and stumble over my words, and then finally sit back down, my face red and flushed.

History isn't any better—it just makes me remember that I only have two days left to finish the World War I paper I've barely begun.

Mostly I wonder how Mom is doing at work and if she's feeling OK. It was weird that morning, getting ready for school like it was any other day, when it wasn't at all like any other day our family had ever had. I couldn't have been the only one in our house feeling miserable, but I didn't want to ask and upset Mom or Chance, especially with Mom trying so hard to act normal.

At lunch Makayla is already sitting at our regular table, along with Emily and Autumn. They're all whispering, heads almost touching, their clothing a riot of pretty colors and patterns. I'm glad Makayla got here before me. Unlike Makayla, who can jump from one friend group to the next without it stressing her out, I still feel a little shy with both Autumn and Emily. We've only been sitting with them for a few weeks, and it takes me a while to warm up to people.

"Josephine, finally! Where were you?" Makayla says, but before I have a chance to answer, she adds, "Never mind." She moves over, pulling my arm to get me to sit down next to her. She smells like cotton candy from her favorite lotion, which she's obsessed with.

"We're talking about my party," Autumn whispers. She leans forward more, turning her head left and right, her long blond ponytail flicking side to side. "Do. Not. Make. Any. Plans. For. October. Tenth. *None!* Oh, and I convinced my parents to let me invite boys too."

"Oh, awesome!" Makayla says, all excited.

That isn't a big deal to me. Because of Chance, I hang out with boys all the time. Newsflash: They're almost entirely idiots.

Emily giggles and tugs the sleeves of her black shirt down over her wrists. "Actually, each of us gets to invite one boy we like. It's a couples party, you know?"

I don't know, but I smile and nod like I do.

What couples? None of us are dating anyone. There are only a few people "going out" in seventh grade, which basically means they hang out during study period together or sometimes after school, and sit together when a group of people goes to the movies or a school dance. Mostly they just text each other a lot.

"Anna's invited too, so that makes a total of ten. Each of you tell me which boy you like, and I'll invite him. If he likes you back, he'll come. If not, um . . . I don't know. I haven't figured that out yet. Maybe you ask a different guy?" Autumn says, chewing on her bottom lip. "Let's hope they all say yes. That would suck otherwise."

I look over at Makayla. This isn't like any party either of us has been to before. I'm nervous at the prospect of inviting a boy to go with me. This isn't a huge party where I can blend in. If there are only ten of us, I'll be on the spot to be all clever and witty. Ugh!

On the outside, I try to look calm, but inside I feel like one of the penguins from that animated movie where the penguins don't want to do something so they keep walking backward, smiling and waving like everything is fine, until they can race out of the room.

I already know Makayla will want to invite Noah Boseman. She's liked him ever since he got glasses last spring. They made his eyes stand out, and Makayla decided he had the nicest eyes of any boy in the whole grade and that his expression "said words without speaking."

Me, though? The only boys I've thought are cute haven't seemed to know I was alive, and since the Ethan Gallagher situation, I've steered clear of anything crush-related. Who needs the trouble? Plus all the boys in our school are friends with Chance and mostly they just annoy me.

Except for one: Diego Martinez.

Diego is less gross than the other boys, which doesn't sound like much of a compliment, but I mean it in the best possible way. He's the opposite of gross. He has two younger sisters he babysits for. I've seen Diego with them at the park, and he's really nice, pushing them on the swings and playing catch, even though the younger one drops the ball every single time. It's totally sweet. And Diego doesn't make disgusting jokes about farts or girls' bodies like some boys at school do.

The best part about Diego is how he always looks like he's been running around. His cheeks are always rosy, and his jet-black hair is tousled and windblown and messy. It's adorable.

But Diego is one of my brother's very best friends, so no way am I letting anyone hear me say anything about him out loud. Otherwise it might get back to Chance. At best, he'd tease me about it or try to be helpful and tell Diego I have a crush on him or something equally mortifying. And at worst he'd be upset with me. He and Diego are tight, and Chance likes things simple and uncomplicated. My liking his good friend is anything but.

So I've been keeping this top secret, barely even admitting my crush to myself. I learned my lesson with the Ethan Gallagher situation.

Never again.

Just hearing about the party makes my stomach feel all churned up, the way it felt when Mom talked to us last night. I thought Autumn was going to have a slumber party—granted, a fancy one, but still, not like a boy-girl party. What's so bad about nail art, pizza, and watching a scary movie?

"Maybe we should have games," Emily says, applying a fruity-smelling lip gloss and rubbing her lips together. She pouts and makes little kissing noises.

Everyone—including me—stares blankly at her.

She sighs. "You know, like kissing games! I found this app that rates your kissing skills. It says I'm an eight out of ten."

Autumn and Makayla start laughing. "Ohmigod, that's so crazy," Makayla says, giggling. "You made out with your phone."

"Come on, gross! Of course I didn't." Emily shakes her head. "But it's kind of funny, right?"

"Spin the bottle for sure," Makayla says, taking her water bottle and giving it a twirl.

I smile again, pretending like this is all no big deal. Underneath the table, I twist my hands together.

"Josephine, Chance is sooooo funny," Autumn says, sticking her spoon into her yogurt and examining the pink contents of the container very, very closely. Still not meeting my eyes, she adds softly, "Do you know if he likes anyone?"

Of the many things Chance and I *do not* talk about, who he does or does not have a crush on is the top of the list.

I shake my head. "Sorry, Autumn, I really have no clue what Chance's deal is."

"I was thinking that maybe he'd want to come to the party? Like, you know, if he knew I liked him?" Autumn's cheeks get as pink as her yogurt, and she pats down the fuzzy blue strands on the arm of her sweater, still looking away. "Will you ask if he likes anyone at school?"

Of course! I think as soon as she says it. Of course, in the magical land that Chance inhabits, Autumn, one of our grade's most popular girls, likes him! Girls always think my brother is mysterious and intriguing and all that march-to-the-beat-of-your-own-drummer stuff.

Apparently they don't realize that this is the boy who once spent an entire weekend trying to teach himself to twirl a pencil between his fingers instead of doing his homework. That seems less mysterious and more like bad time management if you ask me.

"I'll see what I can find out from him," I say, hoping Chance doesn't like some other girl. Otherwise the whole party thing will be *so* awkward, and I'll probably get disinvited.

"Be subtle!" Autumn looks at me nervously. I am happy I'm not the only worried one here. If Autumn is anxious, everyone else probably is too.

"I will, I promise," I tell her. "I'm all about subtle."

"I'm asking Noah," Makayla says. *"Obviously.* So none of you get any crazy ideas about him! What about you, Jo?"

All three of them turn to stare at me.

"Oh. Uh. You know, I'm not sure. I have to think about it," I mumble.

"Maybe you should ask Garrett," Autumn suggests. "He's a really good swimmer."

"Or Jacob!" Emily adds.

"Which one? Jacob K. or Jacob T.?" Makayla giggles.

"Ewww," Autumn says, "Jacob K., obvs! Jacob T. is gross."

"Whoa! Slow down, I'm not sure," I put my hands over my face and close my eyes. "Autumn, when do you need to know?"

Autumn shrugs. "In a few days? Oh! Also my mom said that you can all come over earlier the day of the party, before the boys show up. She'll order us lunch and stuff."

I nod my OK. I thought Autumn's party was going to be low-key. Well, low-key Autumn style, but still. Now it's something I'll have to spend energy thinking and worrying about, which I so don't need right now.

First I have to figure out which boy to ask. Then I have to stress about whether or not he'll say yes. *And* see if my phone thinks I'm a good kisser. And what about Mom? I don't feel right sitting here making plans. What if she needs me that day? I don't want to leave her alone without anyone to care for her.

Who else will keep her company if I don't?

Still, kissing someone for the first time would be . . . actually, I'm not sure what it would be, but it seems like it might be fun. I hate to get my hopes up after the whole Ethan-kickball nightmare, but liking a boy *and* having him like me back would be awesome.

Particularly if the boy is Diego.

4

On the bus home, Chance sits with Oliver, his baseball teammate. But about halfway through our ride, Chance comes and throws himself down next to me, his knobby knee knocking into my pen so it slashes a bright blue line across my math worksheet.

"Chance!" I'm annoyed, even though I know he just can't help it. I put my notebook back into my bag, safely away from him, and take my headphones off.

"Hey," Chance says, his face serious.

"What's up?" I ask.

"Mom's up. I'm freaking out, you know? Sorry I was weird after Mom told us, but I couldn't deal."

I knew Chance was worried. We didn't talk at all last night. He didn't even come out of his room, except to eat a silent dinner with me and Mom, and he hardly touched his food.

That was OK. I didn't feel like talking, either. I still don't.

"*Shhh!*" I hiss, looking around to see if anyone is listening to us.

"*Shhh* what? It's not a *secret*, Jose," Chance says, making a face and using the nickname for me only he uses.

"It *is* a secret, Chance," I whisper, hoping he'll keep his voice down. I take a deep breath. I've been thinking about this nonstop since last night. "Remember how *everyone* talked about us when Mom and Dad split up?"

"Uh, no, not really."

"Well, that's because you're clueless. But people totally talked."

"Who cares?" Chance shrugs, his thin green T-shirt bunching up around his shoulders. It looks like he's almost outgrown it.

"I cared, and Mom cared. I'm sure of it. Who wants people to know more about you than you do about them?"

Chance gives me his "What's your point?" look. I hate that look!

I keep going. "Mom's personal business is private. Do you really want everyone to be bringing over casseroles and stuff like they did with Mrs. McHugh when Mr. McHugh died?"

"Jose, I have no clue what you're talking about. Like you'd ever eat a casserole unless someone had a gun to your head. Remember the tater-tot incident?"

I cringe. When I was seven, I threw up after being served a tater-tot casserole at Aunt Nora's house, and Chance still won't let me live it down.

"Chance!" I hiss. "Not us. The McHughs. Remember? Everyone was staring at Deborah and Kira when they first came back to school. I don't want pity, or strangers bringing us food, or being a charity case. And I know Mom wouldn't either. Have you told anyone yet?"

Chance shakes his head. "No. I haven't. I mean, it felt strange to bring it up at lunch when everyone else was talking about the science test and the Giants game."

I know exactly what he means. I couldn't get up the nerve to tell Makayla about Mom, let alone drop the word *cancer*, like some kind of bomb, into our lunch table conversation about playing spin the bottle.

"But that's why I'm talking to you now," he goes on, softly. "Because, come on, isn't this freaking *you* out too?"

I look around again to make sure no one is listening in and put my finger over my lips in a silent "Be quiet" gesture.

Chance rolls his eyes and whispers, "Fine. I won't say anything to anyone. But why do you always care so much what people think? Seriously. It's like you care more what people might say about you than about Mom having cancer."

I draw in a breath, shocked. I can't believe he said that.

Chance looks down at his gray sneakers. He got a new pair a few weeks earlier for back to school. They're already all dirty and scuffed up, and there's a stain on one that looks like mustard. But even though he's wearing the guilty expression he gets when he does something wrong, he doesn't take it back.

We're silent as the bus lurches along, the rest of the kids yelling loudly and standing up and sitting down and standing up again and hanging over the seats in front of them until our bus driver, Mr. Mike, screams, "SIT DOWN NOW!" from behind the steering wheel. I watch out the window as the houses get smaller and smaller and driveways begin to be marked with simple, hand-painted mailboxes instead of fancy iron gates.

Normally Chance and I understand what the other is thinking, even if we rarely feel the same way about things, but today the silence between us feels thick and dark, muffling our ability to understand each other.

I think about reaching my hand over a few inches and patting Chance on the arm, but I can't do it. I'm too angry about what he said to me. The only thing I can do is sit still and stare straight ahead, arms crossed, mirroring his body language exactly—even down to the furious scowl.

When the bus slams to our stop, jerking everyone forward, Chance jumps up and storms off and into our house without looking back once to see if I'm keeping up with him.

5

Mom told us that she wouldn't be home until five o'clock today, her usual time, but when I get inside, I can hear her on the phone in the kitchen. I pop my head in, and she wipes her eyes and waves to me distractedly, then turns her back and starts talking again in a quieter voice.

I decide to wait for her in the hallway.

"Why is Mom home?" Chance asks as I come up behind him. He looks as nervous as I feel.

I shrug and glare at him. "Now you're talking to me again?"

He glares back. We stand silently in the hallway, hovering near the door, trying to listen in, but I can't make out what Mom is saying.

I just hope there isn't more bad news.

Then we hear Mom getting louder as she walks closer to the kitchen door. "I love you too," she says. The swinging door pushes open.

"Hi!" she says, far too brightly. "That was Aunt Nora. She sends her love to you both."

"Why were you crying?" Chance asks. "What happened?"

"We were talking about my diagnosis," Mom says, her voice breaking up. "I'm not worried about me. I know I'm going to be OK, but I worry about you two. You've already had the divorce and Dad moving to Philadelphia. It's enough already! I just want things to be easy for you for a change. It's not fair."

After that, she's silent for a long time. I try to think of something to say that will cheer Mom up, but I can't. It's hard to act like things will be fine with us unless we know for sure she'll be OK. Because if she isn't OK, I won't be either.

The house is so quiet that I can hear the ticking of the old grandfather clock we have in our living room. It never has the right time, but it keeps trying to catch up anyway.

"But I'm all right," Mom finally says, glancing at us. "And Nora is going to spend a whole week here after I get out of the hospital. Isn't that nice of her?"

"Did you say the hospital?" I ask. I wish we weren't all standing around the door, huddled together awkwardly. "I thought you weren't sure what the next step is."

"I had another appointment today with Dr. Chernoff, and I got a lot of good information from her. She said that because of the size of my tumor, it seems like I'm a candidate for just removing one breast, instead of both."

I look at the front of Mom's shirt—it's hard not to when she said *breast*.

"I'll go in and have that procedure done, and afterward we'll discuss what comes next. But my procedure is first."

"Surgery, you mean," Chance says, leaning back against the wall and kicking at it with his foot.

"Stop doing that." Mom swats at his leg. "Yes, I mean surgery, but it's not the most major surgery. I'll only be in the hospital a night or two, and I should be up and about soon after it's over."

"So how come Aunt Nora is spending an entire week here?" I ask.

"She thought it would be nice for all of us, honey." Mom smooths my hair off my face. "She's going to lend a hand in case I'm feeling tired, and it will be a chance for her to spend time with us. I'm looking forward to it."

"I'm not," I snap, my eyes hot and stinging. "It's not like she's coming for a fun visit."

Mom reaches out to me, but I pull away.

"Why are you home?" I say, sounding rude, even to my own ears. I try again. "I mean, how come you're not still at work?"

"I took the afternoon off. I had my doctor's appointment, and I wanted to make some calls and talk to the insurance company to figure out things. And here . . ." Mom walks over to her purse and pulls out two slightly crumpled-looking pink pamphlets with a big, darker pink ribbon on the front. She hands one to me and one to Chance. "I got these for you."

"What's this?" Chance asks.

"Why don't you read it, stupid?" I snap.

"Don't call your brother stupid." Mom gives me a look. "My doctor gave these to me to pass along to you. It's a group for kids like you who have a parent with cancer.

She said that the woman who runs it is a colleague of hers and is smart and good at what she does."

It says:

St. Francis Teen Support Group
So Your Parent Has Cancer
&$#@!
If you are between the ages of 11 and 17 and have
a parent or caregiver who has cancer, there's a safe
space for you.
Our support group meets every Thursday night in
Room 307B from 6–7 p.m.
Get support!
Meet other kids dealing!
Snacks at every meeting!
Teens, come on in and talk it out!

I look up. "Mom, seriously? This sounds awful. 'Teens, come on in and talk it out!'?" I scoff. "Also, we're twelve, not teenagers."

Chance shrugs. "It doesn't sound so bad," he says. "It does say snacks at every meeting."

Mom turns away from us and starts putting dishes from the dish rack away in the cupboards. "Let's play it by ear."

"No thanks." I drop the pamphlet onto the counter.

Chance shoots me an angry look. It's clear from his expression that he's annoyed I'm not being nicer to Mom. I don't have to be his twin to know that.

People are always fascinated when they find out Chance and I are twins. Like, seriously *so* interested. You'd think considering just how many twins there are strutting around these days that the thrill would have worn off, but everyone is always all: "Ooh, can you read each other's minds? Can you feel each other's pain if one of you gets hurt? Do you speak a secret language only you two can understand?"

Or my absolute favorite, "Are you identical?"

The answer to each of those questions is no, no, no, and no, because I'm a girl, and he's a boy. It's not possible to be identical, genius!

People also like to point out how different Chance and I are, as if I don't already know that. It's been that way from the very beginning. When we were born, Mom and Dad couldn't agree on names—like they couldn't agree on most things. Finally they compromised. Mom picked my name, and Dad chose Chance's. I'm follow-the-rules and stay-in-the-middle-of-the-pack Josephine, and Chance is all, well, what you'd expect from a twelve-year-old boy named Chance. *Not* a follow-the-rules type.

Chance definitely got the more exciting end of the deal. Too bad I'm not named Magenta Clementine, which was what Dad wanted. Chance would have wound up as Stuart—Mom's pick. Then he could be the one everyone expects to be responsible.

Except, want to hear something crazy? Chance often acts more responsible than I do, even though I'll never admit that to *anyone*. Like when I'm stressed out, I use what Mom calls "a tone" with her, which she hates. Chance never does that. And any time Mom and I disagree, even a little bit, Chance jumps in to smooth stuff over. Things like that.

I know he was trying to be nice to Mom by agreeing to go to the teen support group, and I know he wanted me to say it too. But right now I can't bear to do one more thing I'm *supposed* to do, like agreeing to go to an awful talking group or pretending everything is going to be OK when no one can guarantee it will be.

6

I stomp off to my room, annoyed about the stupid pink pamphlet and mad at Mom and Chance for thinking I'd even *consider* it. I'm not a joiner at the best of times.

I throw myself down on my bed, then stand up and do it again, harder and face-first. It doesn't hurt. Instead there's a satisfying *whump* that travels all the way down my body each time I hit the mattress.

I'm glad I'm alone. I'll never get over the feeling of relief at being able to shut my door and be by myself. When Chance and I turned nine, I cried to Mom about how awful it was to share a room with my brother, so Mom got our handywoman neighbor to put a wall in the middle of one of the two bedrooms in the house so that Chance and I could each have our own room. My space is a sliver of a room, much smaller than anyone else's room I know, but it's all mine. It's crazy how much I love my bed and the feeling of the cool bedspread against my body. I love my red swirly paisley patterned sheets and the small white desk and the heart-shaped rug Mom got at IKEA and how I can hang up a poster of Solar Wind above my bed and not have to negotiate over it with Chance.

After I jump on my bed a few more times, I try reading, but I just keep reading the same sentence over and over again. No matter how hard I concentrate, the meaning of the words doesn't travel from my eyes to my brain. I briefly debate doing my homework, but I can't bring myself to. Finally I give up and entertain myself by staring at my bedspread up close, squinting one eye and then the other in tiny slits to create crazy patterns. When I squint just right, the paisleys seemed to come together and make a circle.

Last summer we lost power during a big rainstorm, and I remember wondering when we'd get our Internet and phone reception back. I kept waiting and waiting, feeling aimless and out of sorts. I feel the same way now—waiting for *something* to happen.

The longer I lie on my bed, the angrier I get with everything—and everyone.

"Stupid, stupid, stupid," I mutter, not even sure who or what I'm talking about.

Suddenly my cell phone rings. It's Dad. *Yes!* He's the only person in the world I want to talk to. He knows about Mom, so I don't have to keep anything a secret, and he has this way of making me laugh and cheering me up whenever I'm sad. Probably because Dad never worries about anything. It's contagious.

I swipe to pick up the call. "Hi, Dad," I say.

"Hey, kid. Got time to chat with your old man?"

"Dad, you're not old. Not *that* old, I mean."

"So how's it going?" Dad asks, sounding cheerful.

"Um, OK, I guess."

There's a pause. Then Dad says, "Your brother thought maybe you had some stuff you wanted to talk about?"

I can feel my smile slide off my face. I thought Dad had called on his own to see how I'm doing. Instead he's calling because Chance *told* him to. Chance always tries to butt in and fix things for me, even when I don't want him to. *Especially* when I don't want him to. Like the time

Makayla and I got into an argument and stopped speaking to each other. Chance stole my phone and texted her to apologize, pretending to be me. By the time I figured out what happened, she and I had made up.

When I confronted him, Chance said he felt bad that I was so bummed out. But that didn't make what he did OK.

I should have known he was behind this too. Ever since the divorce, Dad calls once a week to talk to us: Sunday nights between seven and eight. Otherwise, we text each other.

I almost don't want to tell Dad I'm upset, just out of spite, but the words: "It's everything with Mom" come out of my mouth before I can hold them back.

"I know. It's . . . it's crap news, Josephine," Dad says. "There's no way around it. Total crap news."

"It's awful!" My voice breaks. "And Mom said I have to go to a support group!"

"A what?"

"There's a group at the hospital for teens whose parents have cancer. Mom wants Chance and me to go so we can go talk about it."

Dad laughs. "I wouldn't want to go either."

I knew Dad would have my back about that. Back when he and Mom were still married and fighting all the time, I overheard her trying to get him to go to a marriage counselor together. At the time, I didn't even know what a marriage counselor was, but Dad was completely, one-hundred percent opposed. He just kept saying, "I am who I am," and "I don't want to talk to a stranger about my personal business," and "I keep my own counsel."

That made complete sense to me at the time. I didn't understand why Mom couldn't get it. It's only recently that I've wondered why Dad didn't want to stay married enough to try.

I sigh. "I bet Chance goes, and then Mom will make me go with him."

Dad makes a humming kind of sound before pausing, like he's searching for what to say next. "Let's not panic and put the cart before the horse."

"I'm not panicking. I just want . . ." I fall silent.

What I *want* is for everything to be normal—like it was a few days ago. Mom not sick. Me and Chance getting along. Hanging out with Makayla at chess club, instead of having to worry about asking a boy to go to a party. Or even normal as in before the divorce, when Dad lived with us in Westchester, not two hours away in Philadelphia.

That seems like a lifetime ago.

"I wish you were here," I say, sniffling.

Dad is quiet.

"I mean, I'm fine," I race on. I'm not up for hearing—again—why it's impossible for him to move back to be closer to us and about how expensive Westchester is, especially on a musician's salary. "I'm *totally* fine. I just meant it would be cool to see you."

I know even that's a stretch. Chance and I don't have a set schedule for visiting Dad. It used to be every other weekend. Dad would drive up Friday afternoons and pick us up right after school, and the three of us would drive back to Philly. Then we'd do the reverse on Sundays and be home in time for dinner with Mom. But then things got busy with our lives. I didn't want to miss out on stuff like slumber parties, and Chance had games all over the place for soccer and baseball, and Dad started picking up more gigs on the weekends and didn't have anyone to watch us when he stayed out late.

Now we see him less, maybe once a month, plus school vacations. It doesn't feel like enough, but I try not to make him feel bad by saying anything about it. Besides, when we do go to his apartment, I feel guilty leaving Mom home all alone. Dad has his girlfriend and band members and his whole extended family nearby. The only people Mom has to keep her company are Chance and me.

"Ah, I know, sweetheart." Dad sounds regretful. "I'd come visit, but I don't want to overwhelm your mom right now, and my being there might throw her off her routine. I'll be up there soon enough."

He doesn't say it, but I know he means while Mom is in the hospital. Not exactly the type of visit I can look forward to.

"It's OK, Dad," I say, tracing a paisley swirl with the tip of my finger.

"How are your classes? How's chess? How's band?"

"Fine." I sigh. I wish Dad would say something magical that would make everything OK, but he doesn't. We're both quiet. Finally I say, "I should go. I have to catch up on all my homework, or I'm going to be late handing it in."

"OK, Josephine. Remember, I love you."

"Me too." It comes out scratchy because my throat is so tight. I squeeze my eyes shut to stop the tears.

"Honey, I'll call you soon to see how you are. And you can call me anytime. Except remember, I have shows starting at eight and eleven these days, so if I don't pick up in the evenings, that's why."

"Sure, Dad. I know."

"Bye, baby."

I hang up and drop the phone on the floor. Normally Dad can cheer me up no matter what. Not this time.

I take a few deep breaths in and out, just like they taught us in the after-school yoga class I took last spring. Makayla and I made fun of it because the teacher kept talking about "listening to your inner light" and our "sacred journey," but I really liked how at the end my body felt still and at peace.

But no matter how many deep breaths I take, it doesn't work. I still have that dark, scary feeling in my body, like when you're reading a book and your favorite character dies without any warning, or when something goes wrong and you can't fix it, no matter how hard you try.

7

I know I've hidden out in my room long enough. It's been over an hour with no word from Chance or Mom. I figure it's about time that Mom is going to come find me and make me come to the table for dinner—or even worse, "to talk." I take a final deep breath and open the door so I can beat her to the punch.

I creep down the carpeted hallway, drawing out how much time I have alone. This isn't Hogwarts; it's not like we have a huge house with endless nooks and crannies and corridors, so after about eight seconds of tiptoeing, I'm at the doorway to our living room.

That's when I notice Diego sitting on the couch next to Chance, playing a video game.

I step quickly back into the hallway before they notice me, a tiny flutter of excitement in my chest. *Where did he come from?*

For a moment, I wonder if Diego heard about Autumn's party and knows I'm thinking about inviting him. But I haven't told anyone—not even Makayla—about my crush, so unless he's a mind reader, that isn't possible.

I silently backtrack to the kitchen, which is warm and smells like yummy garlic bread. Mom is standing at the stove, stirring tomato sauce and wearing her old, faded red-and-white checkered apron.

"Mom," I whisper over the sound of the kitchen vent fan. "Why is Diego here?"

Mom looks at me funny, probably because Diego comes over a lot. It's not all that weird to see him on our couch, playing *NBA 2K*.

"The same reason he's always here. To visit your brother," she says, getting a spoon from the utensil drawer and dipping it into the sauce. She blows on it, then hands it to me. "I think they're studying for their science test."

Apparently Mom doesn't realize you don't study for a test by playing a video game.

"No thanks." I wave her spoon away. "It looks too hot." I burned myself a few weeks ago on hot chocolate—my tongue and the roof of my mouth were sandpapery for days—and swore that I'd never again eat or drink anything that wasn't lukewarm or colder.

Mom shakes her head, then takes a taste and adds more salt to the pot. "Can you take the bread out of the oven, or are you concerned about catching fire as well as burning your mouth?" she asks me, laughing at her own joke.

"Very funny, Mom." I grab a pot holder and open the oven door. A blast of steamy, warm air hits me, familiar and comforting. Mom has a mealtime routine, regardless of if it's May or November—Wednesday night is Italian night at the Doukas household.

Chance and I tease Mom about it, but secretly I love knowing what to expect. That doesn't make me sound very exciting, but it's true. What's so crazy about liking things to be stable? Surprises are the worst.

Besides, I love garlic bread.

I open the cupboard and pretend to be searching for a glass with laserlike focus. With my back to Mom, I ask, "Is Diego eating dinner here?"

"Oh, good question. Go invite him," Mom says, shooing me with a towel, oblivious to how much I do *not* want to do that.

Wait, actually I do *so* want to do that.

I go back to the living room, making sure my shirt isn't bunched up or my bra straps aren't showing or anything else embarrassing.

"Chance!" I shout over their game. "Mom wants to know if Diego is eating with us tonight."

Chance ignores me, but Diego looks up and gives me a friendly smile. "Tell your mom I said sure, that'd be great," he says.

I smile back before I can stop myself. "OK! Awesome!"

I casually back out of the room—as slowly and calmly as possible—until I get to the hallway. Then I race back into the kitchen, skidding to a stop on the linoleum floor in my bubblegum-print socks.

"Diego says he's eating here," I tell Mom, feeling my face get warm.

She peers at me. "Why are you so red?"

"It's hot in here!" I protest, even more embarrassed that she noticed.

Mom reaches into the cabinets and hands me a stack of plates. "Can you please set the table?"

"But it's Chance's turn to set the table," I whine.

Mom shoots me an exasperated look. "Josephine, just do it."

"Fine. But then he has to do the dishes."

Mom chooses to ignore me.

As I set the table, I think about Chance. I hope he'll keep his word and not say anything about Mom. I want to have a normal meal, even though it feels strange that Diego is having dinner with us. Not *strange* strange. He's eaten at our house tons of times before, but this will be our first meal *together* since I heard about Autumn's party plans.

"That's it, we can eat," Mom says as I'm finishing up. "I'll go tell the boys."

Suddenly I have a panicky realization—Mom probably doesn't know that I asked Chance not to tell anyone what's going on.

"Mom, wait," I say. "I'm not sure Diego knows about you."

"Knows?"

"About your . . . with the . . ." I trail off.

"Cancer," Mom finishes for me. "It's OK. I don't mind if Chance wants to talk about it with his close friends, Josephine. I'd never want either of you to keep your worries bottled up."

"But still, it might be weird to discuss it during dinner, right?" I say, hoping she won't be angry with me. I am a big fan of bottling, and she knows it.

"Right," Mom finally agrees after a long pause. She gives my elbow a squeeze. "No talking about me during dinner. I promise." Then she yells down the hallway, "CHANCE! DINNER'S READY!"

Chance and Diego don't reply, but they materialize in the kitchen a few seconds later.

"It smells good, Mrs. Doukas," Diego says. "Can I help?"

Mom gives Chance a look like, *See?* Then she turns to Diego and replies, "That is very nice of you." She's always on us about being good guests.

"He makes us all look good, Mom," Chance says. "It's like how Dad says a rising tide lifts all boats. Diego is the tide, and I'm the, uh, dinghy!"

Mom shakes her head at him. "Why don't you lift a few platters and serve, then?"

I giggle, and Diego smiles at me.

He sure is smiling a lot, I think. *Hang on, was he always this smiley with me?* I suddenly can't remember.

Plates filled, we all sit down at the table, and Chance and Diego start talking about something to do with their science teacher. I take my cell phone out of my pocket, putting it on silent because we have a no phones during mealtimes rule, and tuck it under the table so I can secretly text Makayla with one hand.

Diego is here, I write.

There's a nanosecond pause before Makayla texts back:

Yeah, so?

So hes cute

GASP!

cut it out

I KNEW IT!

knew WHAT?

I knew he was meant for you!!! I've been saying that since forever

Ummmm no you haven't

Have

Fine u r a genius

Don't you mean A LOVE genius?

Now what do i do?

Now put away your phone and flirt w him!

I almost choke on a bite of garlic bread. **NO!** I type,
here with mom and chance.

ew not good forget that

don't tell anyone!!!!!!!!!!!!!!!!!!!!!

I won't, I promise!

"Honey, didn't you have him as your science teacher
last year?" Mom asks.

Guiltily, I shove my phone back into my pocket and
look up. "What, Mom?"

"I said, didn't you have Mr. Rubenstein?"

"Um. Uh . . ."

Chance, Diego, and my mother are all looking at me,
waiting for an answer.

"Yes! Yes, I had him. Totally!" I smack my forehead
dramatically, laughing super loud. "Looks like I'm having
a senior moment."

Everyone just stares at me. *Awkward.*

"He's pretty nice," Chance says to Mom.

"You say that about everyone," Diego says. "Oh, the devil? He's a cool dude once you get to know him."

I laugh again—normally this time, thank God. That sounds just like something Chance would say.

Diego elbows Chance. "See? Josephine and I know not to trust you. Name someone you don't think is 'pretty nice.'"

Chance concentrates on coming up with a name. "Um . . ." His perplexed expression changes to happiness. "Thanos!"

Diego wads up a napkin and shoots it at Chance. "Thanos isn't a real person. He doesn't count."

Chance throws the napkin back at Diego. "Ultron!"

Diego bats the napkin back. "Nope, try again."

Now that the focus is back off me, I have time to check out Diego. His hair is all gelled up and spiky, and so black it looks almost blue, and he's wearing a long-sleeved black T-shirt with a solid gray short-sleeved one on top.

Why didn't I wake up to the undeniable fact that Diego was super solid crush material years ago? He's objectively cute! And nice! It's so obvious, although just as glaring is the fatal flaw in my crush logic: Diego and my brother are tight. And liking one of Chance's best friends is weird and awkward all around. How could I ever tell if he was hanging around because he liked me or because he wants to hang with Chance?

While I daydream about Diego and wonder what he thinks about me—or if he even does—Chance and Diego power through the meal. Before I know it, they shovel in their last bites, clear their plates, and leave the room in a big blur of legs and arms, and joking and yelling.

When they're gone, it's suddenly very quiet.

"Are you still hungry, Jo?" Mom holds the plate of garlic bread in front of me, looking worried. "You didn't eat that much. Are you feeling sad about . . . everything?"

Mom was entirely wrong about why I didn't eat much. I wasn't sad about her. I was too busy obsessing over Diego. I hadn't thought about Mom's upcoming surgery once during the entire meal. My stomach drops.

I am officially the worst.

Way to be thoughtless, Josephine.

"I'm fine, Mom, really," I tell her, taking a bite of the salty, garlicky bread that I usually love so much. It tastes funny in my mouth, and I stand up to clear my plate.

"You're sure you're OK?" Mom asks me.

"I said I'm fine!" I snap.

Mom looks away for a minute, and I shut my eyes.

"Can I be excused?" I ask, already inching toward the door. I'm suddenly desperate to get back to my room.

Mom waves me off, and I walk away, feeling confused and out of sorts. I zigzagged from grumpy to excited to stupid to mean, all within the time it took to eat a half plate of pasta. It makes me wonder why I even came out of my bedroom in the first place.

8

Even though I went to sleep stressed, I wake up psyched. Now that Makayla knows I like Diego, we have something *major* and *fun* to talk about. And I don't have to feel like I'm keeping a secret from her—at least not about this.

Just so long as she keeps her promise not to tell anyone else how I feel.

I like to keep my crushes a secret from most people. I worry talking about them too much will jinx it somehow, like with Ethan last year. At first I only told Makayla I liked him, which was fine, but then I went to a slumber party at Michelle Parry's house with a bunch of other girls in our grade. We had to list the ten boys we thought were the cutest in order of most to least, and I wrote ETHAN ten times on a sheet of paper, in bigger and bigger letters, so then all the other girls knew too. And then *they* told people.

Instead of asking everyone to zip it, like I should have, I got into the drama of finally being at the center of the story, rather than a supporting character, and talked about Ethan more and more. After months—which felt like *forever*—I discovered he liked me back. It was all anyone could talk about. It was really, *really* huge news.

For a week.

By then *everyone* in our whole grade knew I was obsessed with Ethan. Once he made it crystal clear he was no longer crushing on me, all I got for all that build-up was public humiliation and heartbreak.

Imagining that scenario playing out again is enough to give me hives.

The bus is late picking me up, so I don't have time to find Makayla before the first bell rings, and we don't have time between morning classes to say more than a quick hello. When lunchtime rolls around, I search for her outside the cafeteria, but when I don't see her, I get in line for food, where I'm forced into the tragic choice of meatball sub or egg salad.

Tray in hand, I look around the tables for Makayla and spot her standing, one knee perched on a bench, smiling down at Noah. He's laughing at something she's saying and seems awestruck.

I know for a fact that no boy has ever looked at me like that. I would have noticed the waves of hero worship rolling off him.

I don't approach them, because I don't want to interrupt Makayla mid-flirt. Instead I hang back by the utensil and napkin area and act like I'm getting something, all the while watching them out of the corner of my eye.

I should be happy for my best friend, but I can't help feeling like a big ball of mad. Makayla is so good at talking to anyone without getting shy or flustered, and she looks über-confident next to Noah. Not at all weird. She's always like that with boys, which is probably one reason—along with her being pretty and fun to be around—that so many of them have crushes on her.

I wish I could be like that instead of awkward and uncomfortable. It's one thing to talk to a boy if you're standing next to each other by accident and a conversation *happens*, or maybe you both play the oboe and are placed near each other during band practice. Or like, Diego and Chance are hanging out at our house. Then it's easy! But I could never get up the nerve to actually approach a boy to *flirt-talk*. Especially a cute one I like. That changes everything.

I've been working hard to act like I'm still standing here for a reason, but I honestly can't fiddle around with the soup spoons any longer. Besides, I'm hungry, so I walk over to Makayla and Noah, taking tiny steps in my fuzzy boots, moving as slowly as possible.

"Hi," I say as I get near them, setting down my tray on the edge of their table.

"Jo!" Makayla gives me a big hug, her soft brown sweater tickling my nose. "Sit with us!"

She sits down, giving Noah a nudge with her hip so he'll move over a bit. They both move to the left so they're sitting squished up against each other, giving me room to sit on Makayla's right side, toward the end of the bench. Almost as soon as I sit, Autumn and Emily and Jacob K. materialize with their trays too. I wonder if they've also been lurking around out of sight.

"Noah's telling me about the time he fell off a lawn-mower," Makayla says, a big smile on her face.

"Hey, I could've been chopped up into little bits, and then you'd be sorry." Noah shoves Makayla's shoulder gently with his own, his cheeks flushed.

"I'd be brokenhearted." Makayla giggles, squeezing his arm with one hand and clutching at her heart dramatically with the other.

How was she so good at this?! I wonder.

Watching my best friend in action makes me feel like a total failure. Diego has been in my house—on my couch no less—and I haven't come up with anything even remotely cute to say. Meanwhile Makayla is all Flirty McFlirtface in the middle of the caf. In front of the whole school!

"Noah, are you coming to Spirit Night tomorrow?" Autumn asks. "The cheer squad will be there."

Makayla looks at me for the first time since I sat down. "You should come too, Josephine. You haven't seen the part of our routine that I helped choreograph."

"Maybe. If I'm not too busy." My voice sounds cold and sulky, even to my own ears, but my jealousy keeps me from being nicer. That sounds petty because it is petty, but I can't seem to stop myself.

Makayla looks surprised. Then she shrugs her shoulders. "OK, come if you want. But Spirit Night is always so fun." With that, she turns back to Noah.

I hunch over my meal. Makayla always comes to my boring band recitals. I'm not sure why I said, "Maybe," like I had something better to do. I don't, and we both know it.

Makayla laughs again at whatever Noah is saying, and he blushes, pushing his sandy brown hair out of his eyes and fiddling with his glasses. I turn to face Autumn to ask about Spirit Night, hoping Makayla will overhear and recognize my interest as a subtle peace offering.

"The girls' volleyball team is having a bonfire barbeque," Autumn explains. "And afterward we have a DJ coming. And a lost-and-found fashion show."

"A what?" I ask.

"You know, the girls' volleyball team and the boys' basketball team are going to wear clothing from the lost and found. If it's yours and you want it back, you have to donate two dollars per item. It's going to be soooo funny!"

Before I can reply, Emily and Jacob start talking to Autumn, so I stare down at my tray and hope lunch will be over soon. Then Makayla nudges me.

"Why didn't you text me last night?" she asks.

"I'm sorry," I say. "My phone was frozen. We were on hold with customer service for like a billion hours."

That's a lie. The truth is I felt too guilty about letting Mom believe I was thinking about her cancer when I was really obsessing over Diego. In an effort to seem less shallow, I turned off my phone and did homework—halfheartedly—before going to bed. I was hoping having less fun would make up for being so selfish.

Makayla makes a face as she pulls her hair back off her face with a mint-green hair tie. "Oh, that sucks! Is it working now?"

"Yeah, it's fine. I had to restart it a bunch of times."

"Do you want to hang out today?" she asks. "I could wait around for you during band practice. We could take the late bus home."

I pull the thumbholes down on my hoodie, covering up my wrists. Going over to have dinner with Makayla and her family sounds super nice. We could talk about Diego and Noah and Autumn's party.

Except that would mean not being home for Mom. It feels wrong to be having fun and being all carefree when she's probably worrying. How thoughtless would I be if I did that? Even wishing I *could* makes me feel awful. What kind of kid wants to be away from their mom when she has cancer?

"I can't tonight." I shake my head, not explaining further.

Makayla gives me a confused look, and I can tell she's hurt. Our friendship is usually so easy—we don't fight or get on each other's nerves like some people who always seem to be mad at their BFFs. We *get* each other.

But Makayla is so focused on Noah. It was supposed to just be us having lunch and talking about boys. Instead it's like I'm invisible. If I think about it long enough, I can almost convince myself that it's *her* fault she still doesn't know what's bothering me, or the reason I can't come over after school, or why Spirit Night seems annoying. My brain is sending me big, flashing, *You're wrong, Jo!* signals, but I ignore them.

"Next time," I add, still looking anywhere but at her.

"Totally," Makayla says, getting up from the table. She gives me a hug and shouts, "Love ya!" at me as she walks away. Noah chases after her, trying to act like he isn't.

9

"So . . ."

Chance and I both freeze, forks halfway to our mouths. Mom hasn't been talking much during dinner—none of us have—so that single word is enough to make us stop mid-chew. Chance probably has the same clenching in his gut that I do.

"My doctor set a date for my surgery. It's October seventh."

"Mom, that's like, super soon," I say. "Why are they doing it so quickly? Is something else wrong?"

Mom shakes her head. "No, no, there's no more bad news, honey. The surgeon's office called and told me they have an opening in her schedule. I think that's the only reason I'm able to get in so quickly."

"What do you mean, you *think*? Doesn't the doctor call to explain why they're doing all this stuff?" I slam my hands down on the table, making my fork rattle on my plate.

Chance shoots me a dirty look, "Relax, Jose!"

"Josephine," Mom says, "don't use that tone with me."

My eyes prickle with ashamed tears. Slipping my hands under the table, I pinch the sensitive part of my hand between my thumb and index finger to stop myself from crying. I only want to make sure she's being taken care of. It's not like she has anyone else to watch over her. But it keeps coming out all wrong.

"I just don't want things to be worse than you're telling us," I say, quietly this time.

Mom shakes her head, making her thin silver earrings wave gently back and forth. The gray streaks in her hair look bright under the light.

Has she gotten *grayer* all of a sudden?

"When have I ever kept a secret from you?" Mom asks.

Oh, I don't know, I want to say. *How about when you and Dad kept telling us that you were just "separating" when both Chance and I knew you'd never un-separate? Dad was packed up and moved out before you even uttered the word* divorce *in front of us.*

Parents think they're so subtle, but they're not.

"Take it as a good thing," Mom continues. "I have health insurance. I found something and saw my doctor immediately. I'm getting treatment quickly. All this is positive."

"Positive only if it's opposite day," I mutter under my breath, pushing my rice around on the thin ceramic plate so it makes a little squeaking sound. The plates are painted with tiny red berries dotted around the edges. I helped Mom pick out the pattern last year because they reminded me of Christmas, my favorite holiday.

Now I look at them and wonder what our Christmases will be like from now on. They've already been cut back from four people to three. What if there are only two of us next year? I blink rapidly to clear the image from my mind.

"October seventh, huh?" Chance says, trying to ease the weirdness between me and Mom. "Wow."

For some reason, that date rings a bell. I feel like there's something I'm supposed to do then—*A test? A project due? A band concert?*—but I can't place what.

"It's a Wednesday," Mom says. "Your dad will come up that day before you get home from school, and he'll stay here until I'm back home."

"When will you be out of the hospital?" I ask. Dad's biggest gigs are on the weekends. He doesn't like to miss even one, because he says there's always another trumpet player waiting in the wings, poised to take over.

My mind races. *What will happen if he can't work? What if he loses the jobs he does have? Will he be able to afford to come get us for our weekend visits? What if he has to move even farther away?*

"I'll be there for at least one night. My doctor said after that we'll see, but I assume I'll be home by Saturday at the latest. Don't forget, Aunt Nora will be here to help us too. Oh, and I meant to tell you earlier, I have a meeting with your school's guidance counselor next week." Mom is already at the sink, putting her dishes down as she adds the last part over her shoulder.

"Wait, what?" I say.

"The guidance counselor. You know, Mrs. Hamburg?"

I know *about* Mrs. Hamburg, but I've never spoken with her one-on-one. Chance on the other hand has had his fair share of time in and out of her office since we started middle school, mostly for his ridiculous schemes, like last year when he started a food fight in the cafeteria. ("I didn't start it, but I FINISHED it!" he kept insisting with great pride.) Or when he came up with the idea to buy candy bars in bulk and resell them for a profit in between classes. No one could understand why the vending machines suddenly weren't seeing any action, until they figured out it was because of my brother.

"Mrs. Hamburg is cool, Jose," Chance says. "I'll put in a good word for you."

Mom bursts out laughing at that, but I groan. "Mom, I don't need to see the guidance counselor."

"I'm going to talk to her, not you," Mom says. "That way she can share everything that's going on with your teachers."

"Wait, what? Mom, no! It's none of their business!" I practically scream.

"Calm down." She holds out her hand as if to ward off any more complaints. "This way, if you and Chance are having any problems getting your assignments done on time, or you want to talk to someone . . ."

"Mom, don't worry about me, I'm fine. AND NO TALKING!" I push my feet up against the table and shove my chair back, even though that really bugs Mom.

Mom sighs. "All right, all right." She seems disappointed in me.

"Actually I could use some extra time to finish my assignments." Chance taps his thumb to his lips, looking thoughtful.

Mom points a finger at him. "This isn't a get-out-of-jail-free card, Chance. Your homework still needs to be done. Mrs. Hamburg will just be there if you need her."

"I don't want her calling me into her office in front of everyone," I say, annoyed that Chance is taking this in stride. I imagine how awkward it would be to be chased down the hall by the guidance counselor as she shouts about cancer.

"She doesn't do that." Chance shakes his head, his shaggy bangs flopping into his eyes. "You are such an amateur."

"Please. Only you would be bragging about being an expert at getting in trouble." I copy his head-shaking movement back at him and make a face.

"That's because I'm so good at it."

Mom yawns and rubs the heels of her hands on her eyes. "Kids, I'm sorry, but I'm tired. Why don't we discuss this another time?"

That stops our argument in its tracks. Chance and I look at each other guiltily. "Mom, we can wash the rest of the dishes," Chance offers.

Mom smiles. "Perfect. I'll just be upstairs, then. I have to pay some bills, and I'd like to go to bed early tonight." She gives us each a kiss on the top of our heads.

"Good night, Mom," I say.

"Yeah, good night!" Chance adds.

As soon as Mom is out of earshot, Chance gestures at the plates. "It's your turn."

"It's so yours," I shoot back. "You and Diego ditched me last night, and I got stuck doing dishes for you."

Chance doesn't respond to that. He just unfolds himself and stands up, hunching his shoulders slightly, like he still hasn't figured out how to handle being tall.

"October seventh seems really soon," he says, picking up his glass and balancing it precariously on top of a piece of uneaten chicken.

That's when it hits me. Not only is October seventh two weeks away, but it's also three days before Autumn's birthday party. That's why the date sounded familiar.

I hadn't even told Mom about the party or asked whether it's OK for me to go. Now it seems thoughtless of me to even bring it up. What am I supposed to say, "Oh, hey, Mom, I know you have a few things on your mind, but instead let's talk all about me."?

Besides, I haven't even been all that sure I want to go to the party in the first place. And I know for a fact I'll be too worried about Mom to go if she's still in the hospital. Some people want to be around others when they're nervous or scared, but not me. I tend to withdraw. Or I just want to be around Mom. There's no way I'll be up for socializing.

But as I imagine missing "the party of the year" and everyone talking about it afterward, I feel sad and left out. And that makes me feel bad too, because I'm still only thinking about myself.

Then Chance yells, "Josephine! I've been saying your name for like ten hours."

I jump. "What?!"

"I said, 'Hand me that pan.'" He gestures toward the stove top with soapy fingers.

I wasn't lying; it *is* Chance's turn to clean up the kitchen. But I stay with him and wipe off the table and counters while he washes dishes, neither of us speaking. I can't help wondering what Chance will say about going to a party when Mom is in the hospital. I wish I could ask him, but I don't know how Autumn would feel about me revealing her secret. Just because she asked me to find out if Chance has a crush on anyone, doesn't mean she wants me blurting out *why* I'm asking or for who. I'm sure she's waiting for an answer, but I've been so distracted that I haven't gotten around to discovering anything.

Despite the silence, for a change I don't feel like going to my room and being alone. Even though there's so much I can't—or don't want to—talk to Chance about, it's still nice to be with someone else. Particularly when that someone else is the only person in my life who understands what I'm going through.

If I were alone in my room, I'd just be worrying about Mom. Or figuring out how to get up the nerve to tell Autumn and the other girls about my Diego crush. Or wondering whether there's even a shot of him liking me back. Or stressing over how I've barely started my history paper.

Not to mention stressing over if Makayla is annoyed about how weird I was during lunch. She hasn't texted me once this evening, which is a bad sign. We always text each other at night, even if it's just to share a dumb video or complain about homework.

I can't think of a good explanation for her silence. Either Makayla is upset with me and ignoring me, or she's forgotten about me entirely and is too busy having fun doing something else.

Neither option is good. Either way means things between us are a mess, just like everything else in my life.

I watch as Chance creates mounds of bubbles as he scrubs the sink full of dishes. It reminds me of a time years before, when our parents were still together but fighting all the time. Chance and I were in the kitchen, trying to pretend that everything was OK as they argued in the next room.

"Why would you book a show that far away when you know how busy this weekend is going to be?" I heard

Mom angrily ask. Dad replied—just as angrily—that Mom never respected his career.

My hand slipped as I was washing a glass, and it shattered in the sink, cutting me. There was a brief moment of stillness, and then both my parents raced in to see why I was crying. By then Chance was crying too, because he always cried when I did.

"This has to stop," Mom said, looking at Dad as she wrapped my hand in a paper towel, which quickly turned bright red from my blood. I needed three stitches at the emergency room that night. The following weekend, they told us they were separating.

10

I can tell something is up the second I get to the cafeteria the next day. Autumn and Makayla are sitting at our usual table, facing Emily and Anna. Everyone is whispering, their heads close together.

Makayla sees me and motions me over, mouthing, "Hurry!"

I make my way over to the table, wondering if they realize how *suspicious* they look to everyone else.

"Jo! Where have you been?" Makayla says as soon as I sit down next to her, her arms waving around excitedly. "Do you have your name?"

At first, I'm confused. I have no idea what she's talking about. "Um, what? My name?"

"No." Emily giggles. "Not *your* name. *His* name. You know, which boy you want to ask to Autumn's party. Today's Friday—time to choose our lucky dudes."

"Right, not *my* name," I say as things click. "*His* name. You know my name already."

Truthfully I was hoping for a case of communal amnesia and that every single one of them would forget about the asking-boys-out thing. I'm dying of embarrassment at the thought of telling them I want to ask Diego. But I'll die a million times if I admit that I'm too chicken to go to the party.

I'll seem like such a freak!

"I'm going to talk to the boys tonight at Spirit Night," Autumn says. "That way if anyone says no, you'll have the rest of the weekend to pick a runner-up."

"I will be seriously bummed if Ryan says no," Anna says, making a freaked-out face. "That would be the worst."

"He'll never say no," Emily tells her. "He's *so* into you."

"No he's not." Anna shakes her head. "Wait, do you really think he likes me?"

Makayla looks at her hands and picks at a piece of her chalk-white nail polish, acting all casual. "Actuaaaaaaally, now that you mention it, I might have hinted to Noah that there's a party happening. Aaaaannndddd . . . asked if he would go with me." A big smile appears on her face as she looks around the table at us.

There's dead silence as our jaws all drop, then a shriek from Autumn. "What?! You didn't! Ohmigod, that is so brave, Makayla. Wait, like, you said that *to his face*? Or did you text?"

"No, I mean, yeah, to his face. It kind of just happened," Makayla answers. "We were in study period, and I just went for it. I didn't say anything about whose party it was or who else would be going, just like, 'Would you want to hang out?'"

"AND?!?" Emily screeches.

"And what?" Makayla says, taking a big swallow of her water bottle. But she has a huge grin on her face, so I can tell she totally knows what Emily is asking.

"And what did he say?" Emily says, almost yelling.

"SHHHHHH!" Autumn and Anna shush her at the same time.

Emily looks around guiltily. "Sorry, sorry!"

"He said yes," Makayla says, beaming.

"I KNEW IT!" Autumn says. "I told you he was into you!"

Everyone else is chattering excitedly, but I don't say anything. I feel . . . bummed. Makayla is supposed to be my best friend. Why didn't she tell me first? Or right away after it happened? I know I've been MIA since Mom dropped her cancer bomb Tuesday night, but still!

And how come every single time Makayla likes a boy he likes her back? It's only been two days since we found out the party is going to be coed, and things are already fantastic and all settled for her? Why is everything so easy for Makayla? And why does it seem like the worse things get for me, the better they get for my best friend?

I stand up abruptly, and four heads swivel over to me. "Um, I'm starving," I say. "I'm getting lunch. I'll be right back, I promise." I can't meet Makayla's eyes when I add, quietly, "That's so awesome about Noah."

Makayla turns back to the other three girls, who all start talking a mile a minute:

"What did he say, exactly? Word for word?"

"Was he psyched?"

"Was anyone else listening?"

I walk away before I hear her answers.

I'm jealous and feeling all weird in my skin, but I wasn't lying. I am starving. Plus the cafeteria is serving cheese quesadillas, which is the best dish they make. I load up my tray and return to the table where the rest of the girls are still sitting, whispering like they're planning a prison break.

"Josephine, good, you're back." The very end of Autumn's blond French braid wiggles side to side as she speaks. "Who's your boy? Pick him! Pick, pick, pick!"

The whole table is giggling. "Pick! Pick! Pick!" they chime in.

I need to stall. Feeling panicked, I shove a giant bite of food into my mouth, pointing to show that I'm chewing and can't speak.

Emily jumps in as I continue my very slow chewing, "So far it's Makayla and Noah, Anna and Ryan, and me and Jacob K." She giggles when she says Jacob's name. "If he doesn't say yes, I am going to be forced to transfer schools and change my identity."

"Hey, um, did you find out anything about Chance and what his deal is? Like, does he like anyone?" Autumn asks. She looks down at the table as she speaks, not making eye contact.

I swallow and shake my head no. To be honest, I've been so focused on other stuff that talking to Chance about his love life hasn't been a priority. Doing dishes last night would have been the perfect moment to do it, but I let the moment pass me by. I didn't want to deal with explaining that we're both invited to a coed party, because then Chance would want to know who my "co" was going to be.

So I lie.

"Autumn, I'm sorry, I hinted like crazy, but Chance was totally clueless, which is no surprise. He's kind of clueless always." I don't feel the tiniest bit guilty for throwing my brother under the bus. It's every Doukas for herself. "Want me to try again later?"

"Yeah, would you? I mean, it's OK to tell him the whole deal. I mean about me and the party and stuff." Autumn is blushing and stumbling over her words. I feel awful for lying and making her wait for something so important. I'm the worst!

"I'll talk to him tonight before Spirit Night," I say. "For real, I promise."

"Thank you!" Autumn leans across the table to give me a hug. She smells fruity. "So, everyone else is set. Seriously, what about you? Don't you like anyone even a little bit?"

Everyone is staring at me.

"It's so hard!" I blush, covering my face with my hands. "So many boys are so dumb. Like, you know, how Garrett is always joking about butts and stuff all the time? And Oliver makes those stupid comments about me and my oboe?"

"Right," Anna nods. "Most boys *are* idiots. Still, though . . ."

"I don't . . . there's no one I really like. . . . I mean, they're all friends with Chance. . . . And no one has a crush on me. . . . I haven't even asked my mom if I could go. . . . What if we have plans that weekend. . . ." I keep talking, rambling on and on, hoping they'll drop it.

The girls all look at me like I'm speaking in a foreign language. They're not letting me off the hook. I have to name a name, or I'm getting axed from the party list and probably setting myself up for long-term social isolation.

I take a deep, slow, long breath, in through the nose, out through the mouth, like yoga teacher Max taught me.

It does nothing to calm me down. *What a crock!*

"Sheesh, you guys are relentless!" I hiss at them. "Fine! Diego! OK? It's Diego!" As soon as his name comes out of my mouth, I drop my head on to the table to hide my mortification, careful not to get a face full of tortilla.

The whole table makes a collective *Ooooooohhhhh* sound.

Makayla claps her hands. "Can you guys believe it? Jo, I honestly had zero idea you liked him before you told me yourself. If you hadn't said anything, I never would have figured it out. I can't believe you kept it a secret all this time."

Oh no.

"Well, it hasn't been that long," I rush to add. "I mean, I'm not *obsessed* with him, he's just the best of the worst. You know, the lesser of all the many evils."

"Uh-huh," Autumn says, nodding all smugly.

"Right," Emily says, sounding equally smug.

"So what you're saying is that you want to make out with him," Autumn says. "I'll be sure to tell him that."

"DO NOT DO THAT!"

Autumn cracks up. "Josephine, I won't. I'm joking! And you don't tell Chance I want to make out with him either, OK?"

"Don't worry. I don't even want to talk to Chance about him *kissing* anyone. Gross!"

"Now what?" Anna asks. "I won't be able to relax until I know if Ryan says yes or not."

"I'll ask them tonight at Spirit Night!" Autumn says. "I'm sure they'll all say yes."

"Yeah, then it's officially a party!" Makayla whoops.

"You're so lucky," Emily says, clutching dramatically at Makayla's shoulder. "You already know Noah is into you. The rest of us have to sweat it out for hours and hours and hours and hours."

Sweat it out is right, I think. I'm sweating just from telling my friends that I like Diego. In a few hours he'll find out too and so will everyone else we're friends with. I'm for sure not going to Spirit Night now.

I pull at the collar of my shirt, trying to cool off, so I won't have to go back to class a big, clammy mess. I tried to play it off like Diego is just someone I can tolerate, but I don't have faith in other people to be subtle about things like that. I hope Autumn doesn't say something really crazy to Diego, like I'm in love with him or I can't stop dreaming about him.

Urk!

Makayla shrugs, a half smile on her face. "I'm just lucky, I guess."

I take another bite of my lunch and try to look as happy for Makayla as everyone else does.

Noah liking Makayla doesn't impact whether or not Diego thinks *I'm* cute. But somehow it feels like there's only a bit of good news to go around, and I'm not going to even get a tiny scrap of it.

11

As soon as I get home from school, I eat, like, six pizza bagels. Not the mini kind either. I don't usually eat breakfast, so lunch is breakfast, and then by midafternoon I'm ready for what a normal person would call lunch. It's confusing.

Mom is still at work, and Chance is at soccer practice, so while I have the house to myself, I brainstorm subtle ways to find out if Chance likes Autumn and whether he'll want to be her "date"—*ugh! that word!*—without letting on that I'm planning to ask Diego to the exact same party. I really want to get Autumn an answer before Spirit Night starts. She's counting on me. She's never asked me for a favor before, and she's being so nice about inviting me to her party. It's important to succeed here.

The success of my plan hinges on one very important thing: Chance only half listening to me. A strong possibility, considering my brother's miniscule attention span.

By the time Chance comes clomping through the front door in his soccer cleats after practice, I'm ready. "Hi, Chance!" I say, leaping up from the kitchen table as he enters the room.

He jumps back. "Jeez, Jose, you scared me. What are you doing, you freak?"

"Nothing. Hanging out. You?"

He gestures to his muddy soccer uniform. "Practice. *Obviously.*" He turns to the refrigerator, his shoes squeaking on the floor.

"Mom doesn't let you wear cleats in the house," I remind him.

He ignores me and grabs the orange juice, taking a huge drink as he stands in front of the open refrigerator.

"She also doesn't let you drink from the bottle."

"This isn't a bottle," Chance says. He points at the olive oil Mom keeps on the counter. "That's a bottle. *This* is a carton."

I roll my eyes. "Shut up, Chance."

"You shut up."

My approach is not going well. *Focus, Josephine!*

"Hey," I say, trying to get back on track. "Do you know Autumn?"

Chance gives me a funny look. I can't blame him. Of course he knows Autumn. We've all gone to school together since first grade. And back when Autumn threw all-grade birthday parties with every kid invited, Chance went to them. He still talks about how her parents had a special restaurant-sized pizza oven built in their giant backyard. Chance is *very* into pizza. He even researched how much it would cost to get a pizza oven for our dinky scrap of yard. It was more than Mom paid for her used car, so sorry, Chance, no specialty pizza for us.

"Anyway, you know her, right?"

Chance sighs.

"She's nice," I add helpfully. "Her parents are . . ."

"Jose! I know her. We've been in Spanish class together for, like, three years running. I know who you're talking about. There's only one Autumn in the whole school. Probably in all Westchester North. It's not the world's most common name."

"I bet there's only one Chance too!" I smile brightly. "So you two have that in common."

"There will never be another Chance," he says. "Now and forever I am the one."

I ignore that, waiting until his back is to me, then say, "Do you think she's cute?"

He pauses for a minute. Then he turns around to stare at me suspiciously. "Why? You taking a poll?"

"Ha ha ha. No, just wondering. I think she's pretty, that's all."

"Yeah, she's OK, I guess." Chance shrugs.

"So, like, if she liked you, would you like her back?"

"What," Chance says slowly. "Are. You. Talking. About?"

"Nothing. I just get the sense that she thinks you're cute is all. I'm just curious."

Chance shrugs again. "Great."

He goes down the hall, squeaking and dropping mud with every step. I follow him into his room and perch myself on the clothing-covered desk chair as he unlaces his cleats. He's either ignoring me deliberately or doesn't realize I'm right there.

Suddenly it hits me. What if Chance doesn't like girls that way?

Our uncle Doug, Dad's younger brother, is gay. He and Dad look a lot alike, but Doug is super responsible and wears a tie every day and has been with his partner—now his husband—since they met in accounting school. Now they run their own tax preparation business out of their townhouse in Philadelphia, and we aren't allowed to visit them during tax season because they're too busy.

I don't want Chance to think that I care if he likes boys instead of girls . . . but it's going to be *so* awkward if he does because that will totally ruin Autumn's entire birthday party plan!

"Chance?"

"Yes?"

"You like girls, right?"

"What?"

"I mean, like, you *like them* like them?"

"Compared to what, liking lemurs?"

"No, you know, all these girls always have crushes on you, and I never know if you like them back that way. It's hard to tell. I mean, we know Uncle Doug is gay because he's married to Uncle Kevin—"

"You mean, like am I gay?" Chance interrupts. "You could just ask. I wouldn't keep a secret like that from you."

I feel a pang of guilt when he says that, mostly because I can't say the same. I'm keeping so many secrets from everyone: from Chance about how I like Diego; from Makayla about Mom's cancer and upcoming surgery; from Mom that I'm thinking about things besides her.

Am I being myself with anyone?

"If you were gay you'd still be annoying," I say, trying to cover up how guilty I feel.

"Right back at you," Chance says, tossing a cleat and barely missing my foot. "I'm not gay, though. But I do think you're exaggerating about all the girls who like me. I don't have a fan club or anything."

"So if Autumn liked you, would you like her back?"

"Sure, yeah, I mean, she's cute and she's nice. And she does have that pizza oven." Chance looks all kinds of embarrassed, and it's normally impossible to embarrass my brother. "Seriously, why are you asking?"

I look at him hopefully. "Do you have to know right this second?"

He shakes his head. "Never mind. But can I get changed in peace, please? It's almost time to go."

"You're going to Spirit Night?" I ask.

"Yeah, aren't you? I thought you were going to watch Makayla. That's what you said last week."

I sigh. "I don't feel like going."

"Because of Mom?"

"What? No. I'm just too tired to go."

"Oh, you're 'tired.'" Chance makes air quotes.

"No, really! I'm probably getting sick." I manage a weak cough and gesture to my throat in what I hope is a frail, pathetic way.

"Jose, it's OK if you're bummed about Mom. I am too."

"I'm not! I mean, I am, but I'm OK. I'm just not in the mood for Spirit Night. Like, all that spirit."

"Yes, I hate when there's too much spirit." Chance rolls his eyes. "That's the worst."

I throw his soccer ball keychain at him, and it bounces off his knee and lands on the floor. "Come on, Chance, you know what I mean! Everyone is acting all excited, but it's just our regular old school. On Monday everyone will be back to complaining about having to be there. Shouldn't the spirit magic last longer than forty-eight hours?"

"Whatever," Chance replies, ignoring my rant. "I have to go tonight. Diego and I got stuck being in the lost-and-found fashion show."

"Diego?"

"Yeah, he and his dad are picking me up."

Diego has to drive by our house on his way to school, so Chance often grabs rides with him, but still! Diego is coming over to *our house*, where I'll be sitting at home, looking like a dork in my pajamas, doing nothing while he and Chance hang out with like, every other kid in seventh grade at Spirit Night.

"I thought it was the basketball team doing the fashion show. Or am I confused?"

"Those guys were too chicken to do it. So Coach Brian asked if Diego and I would help out. We figured, why not? See, here's my Blue Steel." Chance poses his face in a severe, model-like way, and we both crack up.

This is what I mean about it being hard to embarrass my brother. He'll be in a fashion show wearing someone else's old clothing and not care. I'm surprised Diego agreed to do it, though. He's way less weird than Chance. But I guess that's what best friends do for each other. Put up with each other's crazy schemes. Like last year, for example, when Makayla made me enter the three-legged race at Field Day. It was way more fun than I expected it to be, even though we didn't come close to winning. We were laughing too much.

"You could get a ride with us," Chance says. "Diego's dad's truck has a back seat so there's room for four."

I am tempted. Being home with Mom doesn't sound quite as fun as being with everyone at school. And I wouldn't mind seeing Diego in a fashion show. That way I could stare at him as much as I want.

But I have so many better reasons for not going. Makayla hasn't even texted to see if I'm free and want a ride, like she usually does when the cheer squad is performing. She's probably so busy with Noah that she forgot about me. And I have no clue when Autumn is going to unleash her barrage of matchmaking with all the guys. What if she does it in front of everyone? Or like, when a microphone is on? And I have to watch in real time as

Diego freaks out about my liking him and then he avoids me but has to give me a ride home and . . .

I can't stop thinking about the horror of it all. The evening could turn into a nightmare that I won't be able to wake up from.

Public humiliation. Everyone laughing at me.

What was I thinking, telling Autumn that yeah, no big deal, go ahead and tell Diego I want to chill with him at her party?

Gulp.

I feel almost sick imagining how wrong things could go. Getting up, I try to play it off as nothing, telling Chance, "Nah. Next time. Have fun. Text me pictures, OK?"

"See ya."

I shut his door quietly on the way out and try to calm myself down. At least I accomplished one of my most pressing goals: finding out whether Chance likes Autumn back.

I have to tell Autumn ASAP! As soon as I lie down on my bed, I text her: **hola**

She gets back to me right away: hola to u

are you somewhere private?

no wait

There's nothing for a minute, and then she texts me again: now i am. whatsup?

hey i talked to chance

what did you say?

i was sooooo careful & barely said anything

like what

I asked if he knew you and he said you were in Spanish together

then what

then he said you were nice

cool

AND CUTE

NO!!!!

YES!!!!

for real?

for real. he's going to spirit night so you'll see him right?

yes! are you coming?

I can't i think I'm getting sick

Feel better and THANK YOU!!!!! xoxooxoxoxooxo

u r welcome!

ill ask the other guys later ok? Including diego.

eek

no eek. its all good

have fun tonight!!!

see ya!

I hope Autumn will be as low-key with Diego as I was with Chance, but I kind of doubt it. She's much more of a Makayla or a Chance than a Josephine.

I lie down under my covers with the goal of hiding out for as long as I can, praying Chance won't come into my room when Diego arrives. Just in case, I get up and drag my chair underneath my door handle so that no one will be able to open it.

Then I lie in bed, staring at my phone. It sounds crazy considering she's my best friend, but I can't decide if I should text Makayla or not. Finally I text her **GOOD LUCK!!!!!!** and wait to see if I hear back.

Nothing.

It seems ridiculous, even to me, to stay home with nothing to do while everyone else is at Spirit Night, but between the weirdness with Makayla and the potential for total disaster with Diego, I can't work up the nerve to show my face. I make a pact with myself that I won't spend the whole night obsessing about what's happening at school. To show I'm serious, I even turn off my phone and put it in my sock drawer, stashing it underneath a pile of itchy tights, so I won't keep checking it.

"Stay in there," I say to my cell, shoving the drawer shut hard so it knows I mean business.

12

About eight seconds after banishing my phone for the whole evening, I yank it back out of my sock drawer. Mom is home by now, and then I hear the doorbell ring, which means Diego is there. I can hear Mom greeting his father, Mr. Martinez.

"Luis, thank you for taking Chance tonight," she says.

"It is no problem," he replies.

I press my ear harder against my bedroom door, straining to make out anything Diego might say, but I can't hear him.

My phone is still powering back up when I hear Mom shout my name.

I come out of my room, peeking around the corner to make sure Chance and Diego are gone. I have no desire to kick off my weekend with Diego catching me in snowflake-patterned flannel PJ pants and Dad's old oversized Philadelphia Phillies sweatshirt.

"Honey, why aren't you at Spirit Night?" Mom gives me a concerned look.

"I didn't feel like it."

"Chance said something about there being 'too much spirit' for you?"

I roll my eyes. *Chance is such a bigmouth!* "Something like that."

"You don't want to go out with your friends?" Mom asks.

I shrug.

"Well, OK. Do you want to watch a movie? Have you eaten?"

I'm still full from all the pizza bagels I ate earlier. "I'm not hungry, Mom. Thanks."

"Well if you change your mind, I'm going to reheat some leftover minestrone soup. There's plenty."

Mom reaches out and pats my head, which usually bugs me because I'm not a baby. But I let her do it anyway. Then she walks away, and I yank out my phone.

No messages.

Ugh.

I wonder what's happening at school. Has Autumn said anything to any of the boys yet? I text her: **hows it going?**

Then Makayla, even though she didn't reply to my first message: ur going to kill it tonite!

Finally Emily and Anna: are you guys already at spirit night?

Then I sit and stare and stare at my phone, my heart racing.

Finally Autumn texts back: fine

Emily: yeah, all here. where are u?

But from Makayla, still a big, fat nothing.

I write Emily back: **i'm at home. cant come tonight. let me know right away if anything happens. ANYTHING!!!!!!**

I send the same message to Autumn and Makayla. I hope they remember me, sitting all alone at home by myself, while the rest of them are together celebrating and having fun. I'm *not* being dramatic. People forget about you really fast when you're not around!

Mom sits down next to me on the living room couch, balancing a bowl of soup in her hands. "Come on, let's watch something," she says.

"OK," I agree. I might as well. The only difference between sitting alone in my room, staring obsessively at my phone versus sitting on the couch with Mom, staring obsessively at my phone is that at least sitting with Mom makes her happy.

"Here," she says, handing me the remote. "You pick."

"Wow, really? Thanks, Mom."

"Your brother isn't here to make me crazy about your choice, so whatever you want. And I won't say a word, even if you make me watch that terrible movie about the teen talent show overtaken by zombies again."

"Let's watch *Friends*!" I love *Friends*. I'm on my third round of binge-watching on Netflix. I love how much fun everyone has together and how close they are. Nothing tears them apart. I wish I had a Central Perk in my life.

Mom shrugs. "Fine. Anything but singing zombies!"

I giggle, then select an episode and hit play. But a second later my phone buzzes with a text from Autumn: Your brother just got here. are you SURE he said yes?

yes! positive

yes what? yes as in he said yes or yes that you know he's here?

No, i know he's at spirit night. I mean yes I'm sure he likes you. He said so.

Diego is here with him

yeah, i knew that

im asking him for you right now.

WAIT!!!!

Autumn doesn't write back.

On the screen, Phoebe is singing about her smelly cat.

"Josephine, if you're just going to text with your friends, can I watch the news instead?"

"Fine." I don't even look up at Mom when I answer.

My heart is racing. It's been at least forty-five seconds since Autumn's last text. Why is it taking her so long to get back to me? How horribly did her talk with Diego go? Who else is there? Does everyone know what's going on but me? What if me liking Diego was a total joke? What if Chance decided to get involved and be "helpful" in the stupid way only Chance does? What if at the exact moment Autumn went up to talk to Diego, it got super quiet because the sound system turned off, and every single kid in school heard her say that I like him?

Aaaaaacccccckkkkkk!

What was I thinking blurting out "Diego!"? I should have said that I met some random boy online who lived in Canada and that we were too in love for me to even think about hanging out with anyone else.

Arthur. That seemed like a good fake boy name. My Canadian boyfriend Arthur, who liked mooses—or was it meese?—hockey, and me.

I text Autumn again: **Hey**

Still nothing. The pizza-bagel baby in my stomach drops down even further.

I text Makayla instead: **are you with autumn?**

She doesn't write back for a while, then: No. i'm rehearsing a final time for my routine

I immediately feel like a jerk. Helping choreograph a Spirit Night routine is a huge deal. Not only am I not there cheering her on, now I'm distracting her.

Finally! so sorry i am missing your big night. I'm exhausted :(

sokay

Autumn is asking diego now for me!

dont worry

me worry? never!

Makayla knows me well enough to understand my sarcasm, even through text. I stress about stuff *a lot*. Most people don't realize it because I'm a quiet worrier instead of a loud, showy, gasping-and-clutching-my-heart worrier. But it's the same thing inside. I just don't like to discuss it.

Discussing bad stuff never helps. It just makes it worse.

Besides Mom, Makayla is one of the few people who knows how easily I freak out. She never tries to talk me out of it, though. She just listens. I appreciate that. Chance is all, *Don't sweat the small stuff, and it's all small stuff.* He read that on a T-shirt once.

He doesn't seem to grasp that if you want someone not to be anxious, rolling your eyes and saying, "STOP WORRYING, YOU'RE BEING RIDICULOUS!" is about the worst thing you can do.

My phone dings again. It's Autumn this time:

guess what?

what?

diego said cool

cool what?

cool about my party and hanging out with you

are you sure?

sure I'm sure

TELL ME WHAT HE SAID

I JUST DID! HE SAID COOL

No, I mean . . . blllaaaaargh

"Mom, I have to go to the bathroom." I jump up from the couch. I can't text anymore. I need Autumn to give me every single detail, down to Diego's vocal inflections. I'm not sure I've ever spoken to Autumn on the phone before, but this is life and death!

"Why are you bringing your phone if you have to go to the bathroom?" Mom asks me as I walk away.

I pretend not to hear her and shut the bathroom door.

"Hello?" Autumn answers on the third ring. It's loud in the background—music and a jumble of voices.

"Can you talk?!" I yell, hoping she'll be able to hear me.

"Um, it's kind of public, Jo!" she yells back.

"I REALLY NEED TO KNOW WHAT JUST HAPPENED!"

"Hang on, OK?" It stays loud, then suddenly it's quieter on the phone. "Hey, I'm back," Autumn says.

"Where are you?"

"The girls' locker room, so if someone comes in, I'm going to stop talking."

"SO ABOUT DIEGO?" I prompt, hopping up and down nervously.

"Stop shouting! I can hear you now. I told him I was having a birthday party, and that it was me, Makayla, you, Emily, and Anna."

"And?" I say. I'm dying of suspense.

She goes on. "And then I said how each of us could bring a guest, like a boy guest. And would he want to go as your guest."

"Guest?"

"Yeah. *Guest* sounds less stupid than *date*, don't you think?"

I honestly wasn't sure. *Guest* sounds dumb, like a hotel guest, but then again, *date* is the old-timey worst.

"So then what?" I ask.

"So he said, 'That sounds cool.'"

"That's it?"

"That's it. He said, 'Sure, cool.'"

"Wait, I thought he said, 'That sounds cool,' but now you're saying he said, 'Sure, cool.' Which one was it?"

"Hmm." Autumn pauses. "I'm pretty sure he said, 'That sounds cool.'"

"How sure?" I ask. I need answers!

"I don't know, but, Josephine, really, he seemed into it! I promise."

I don't know what to think. Did Autumn make it clear to Diego that her party is like, a *thing*? A date thing? A boy-girl thing? And that I'm the date?

I rub my forehead with my hand. "Um, so thanks for talking to him," I say.

Autumn sounds super pleased with herself. "You are SO welcome! I have to go find Ryan and Jacob K. now, OK?"

"Have you seen Chance?" I ask before she can hang up.

Autumn giggles. "Only for a second. I think he's getting ready for the fashion show."

"Oh—" The call cuts off as I'm still saying goodbye.

I thought once Autumn talked to Diego I'd feel better, like everything would be resolved, but now I wish I'd gone to Spirit Night instead of hearing everything secondhand at home. I can't tell whether to be beyond excited or beyond bummed.

Sometimes overthinking things is a good idea because you don't get taken by surprise. Other times, the only person I outsmart is myself.

13

I hate it when I can't sleep. All night long I keep flipping around in bed, trying to find a comfortable spot—feet out of the covers, feet in, arms underneath the comforter, one arm out—but nothing feels right. Finally I pass out from exhaustion and boredom. The only reason I wake up the next morning is because Chance is thumping and clomping around the house like a rhino. How can someone so skinny be so loud?!?

"Chance, KEEP IT DOWN!" Usually I'm up well before him. All my friends can sleep forever, but I have a hard time sleeping late, even on weekends. My eyes pop open at 6:59 a.m., no matter what.

Seconds later, he knocks on my door. "Jose, you in there?"

"Obviously," I call back to him. "I'm trying to sleep, though. Are you wearing wooden clogs? Why are you making so much noise?"

I hear him laugh, and then he knocks again. I sigh and give up on going back to sleep.

"Fine, come in. What do you want?"

Chance waltzes in and leans against my doorframe, arms crossed. "So I hear there's a party happening."

Oh boy.

As casually as I can, I say, "I already told you Autumn was talking about that, remember?"

"Yeah, but you didn't mention that you were invited."

I shrug. "Huh, weird. I guess I forgot."

"Oh right. You just 'forgot,'" he says, making air quotes around the last word. "You *forgot* to mention it even as we were talking about it?"

"I could have sworn I told you! It must have slipped my mind."

He gives me a look.

"Did she mention who else is coming?" I ask, trying to sound chill. I wrap my comforter around me so only one eye is peeking out.

"She said Makayla and Anna and Emily and you and then some guys."

Why isn't he saying anything about Diego? I think anxiously. "That's it? Did she mention which boys?"

Chance pretends to think, then snaps his fingers. "I think . . . oh yeah, I almost forgot, DIEGO!"

Busted.

My face gets hot. It's beyond embarrassing for Chance to know I have a crush(ish!) on Diego. I don't need him making a huge deal out of it and never letting me live it down.

I think about trying to change the subject, not wanting to die of embarrassment, but Diego and Chance are best friends. Whether I like it or not, Chance is my best hope for finding out if Diego likes me back.

"Did Diego say anything to you? About coming? With me, I mean?" I ask.

"Yeah, he told me after he talked to Autumn. He was here last night picking me up, though. You could have asked him yourself instead of having her do it."

I recoil in horror. "What? You're crazy! I would have seemed totally insane!"

"Why?" Chance seems genuinely surprised. "It's not insane to ask someone to hang out. Why do people make stuff into such a big deal?"

I glare at him through the one eye visible outside the blanket. "I don't have time to explain to you that it's weird to ask Diego to come to some party with me. He barely even knows me."

Chance cracks up. "He's here all the time! He knows you. Also, you're my twin, so he knows you through . . . um, what's that thing? Synthesis? Osmosis?"

"Yeah, because we're so *porous*," I say, making my voice drip with so much sarcasm that it's impossible to miss.

Chance shakes his head. "I don't get it. Why did Autumn have to ask Diego out for you, and why did you have to ask me out for Autumn? That's so complicated!"

"You wouldn't understand," I say. "It's too sophisticated for your immature brain. Look, Chance, it's not a huge deal who asked who or who's going, right? I mean, it's just one night. Friends hanging out. I thought it would be nice to ask Diego since you were going already. It's convenient."

Chance nods, trying to be serious when he's so clearly trying not to laugh at me. "That was very 'thoughtful' of you." There go the air quotes again.

I wish he were close enough for me to kick him in the shin. Instead I ignore him.

That's a trick I learned from Makayla. Her family has a dog—a Labradoodle named Robert (yes, seriously)—that used to bark constantly, like anytime he wanted to play or eat or go out or anything. *Bark, bark, bark.* Makayla's mom finally hired a dog trainer who told them Robert was just looking for attention. Instead of responding, they had to ignore him every time he barked and turn their backs on him until he stopped.

I was there when the trainer was over, and even though they were talking about Robert, it sounded like it made sense for people too. I try to do that with Chance whenever he says something to annoy me. Turn my back and ignore him like he's a dog. Most of the time it seems to work pretty well.

"Did Diego say anything else to you about it?" I ask half-heartedly, knowing I'm unlikely to get any good info out of my brother. He's not the most detail-oriented person, and I can't imagine him and Diego sitting around, sharing in-depth opinions about party invitations.

"Yeah, he said it sounds cool."

Cool?! I think. *Doesn't Diego have any other words?*

"Cool, like the party will be cool? Or that it's cool I'm going? Or cool that Autumn is having a party? Or cool that he's invited? Which part, exactly, is so cool?"

Chance gives me a funny look. "Jose, what do I know? He said 'cool,' we didn't get into some huge discussion about it. We had clothing to model." Chance points down at the faded navy Yankees T-shirt he's wearing. "I got this from the lost and found last night because no one claimed it!"

"That is so disgusting!" I say. "It probably has lice. Or scurvy."

Chance rolls his eyes and leaves my room, shouting, "Scurvy isn't contagious!"

"I knew that!" I shout back.

But as I'm yelling, he pops his head back in, looking genuinely curious. "So wait, do you have a crush on Diego or not?"

I shriek, "GO AWAY! I cannot talk about this with you!"

Chance leaves again, but I can hear him laughing all the way down the hall.

I decide to call Makayla. The fact that she took so long to text me back last night is weighing on me, but I feel awful about not cheering her on the night before. Maybe it's on me to make things right with her, and she's waiting for me to do it.

"Jo!!" Makayla picks up after the third ring, sounding slightly breathless. "What's up?"

"Nothing." I hear giggling in the background. "Where are you?"

"Emily's house. I spent the night, but my mom is picking me up in a minute and we can't seem to roll my sleeping bag back up." I hear another giggle. "Can we talk later?"

The smile slides off my face, and I immediately feel hurt. There is *nothing* worse than finding out about something you weren't invited to. I pretend to be casual, though. "Sure, I was just calling to say hi. I don't really have anything to talk about."

"Oh my God, we have SO MUCH to talk about! I want to know what happened last night with Diego!"

"I don't know what happened! I wasn't even there!"

"Oops, gotta go, Emily's dad is making me extra bacon. Call me later, OK?" She hangs up before I can reply.

Just great.

I throw myself back down on my bed and shut my eyes, the sun making me see orange behind my eyelids. I can't stop thinking about Makayla spending the night at Emily's house. I imagine them staying up late talking, and loneliness settles around me. I know I was the one who decided not to go to Spirit Night, but I feel left out anyway.

When did everything in my life get so confusing? And so exhausting?!

I've just decided to spend the day sulking around my room and feeling stupid for not going to Spirit Night when Mom taps on my door.

"Josephine, what are you doing?" she asks.

"I'm tired!" I yell back. "I'm resting!"

"Tired from what? All that sleeping you did?"

"Ha ha ha, Mom."

"If you don't get up, you're going to grow roots and become permanently attached to the bed."

"FINE! I'm coming!"

I get up, stomp around my room, being extra slammy when putting clothes back into my dresser, and then go into the kitchen to find something to eat. Mom is at the kitchen table, a stack of envelopes, papers, and her checkbook in front of her. She has on the black-rimmed eyeglasses we picked out together, and her hair is still wet from her shower.

"Hey," I say, sitting down across the table from her. "What are you doing?"

She peers at me over her glasses. "Paying bills and filling out insurance forms."

I look over at one sheet of paper. Post-Surgical Care is written in big, black letters, underlined.

I point to it. "What's that for?"

"Oh, that? It's from the doctor's office. It explains what to do after my procedure." Mom tries to casually shuffle the sheet underneath a pile of other papers so I can't see it.

I frown. Time is rushing ahead. Her October seventh surgery date is coming up way too soon. I wish I could slow everything down.

Mom smiles at me, sensing my distress. "Don't panic."

I get up and get myself a bowl of cereal. "I'm not *panicking*, Mom, I'm just not super happy about any of this."

What I don't tell her is that I feel wobbly. And unsettled. Off-kilter. And that I've been feeling that way ever since she told us about the cancer. I want to sit when I'm standing, stand when I'm sitting, talk when there's no one to talk to, and be left alone when I'm surrounded by people.

"I'm in good hands with my medical team," Mom says, interrupting my thoughts. "I have every reason to be confident that I am going to be OK."

I look away from the hospital paperwork and try to focus on something less grim. "Can we have lunch at the diner today?" I ask, hoping it takes my mind off feeling left out of Makayla's sleepover last night.

"Hmm," Mom says, looking down at her pile, then back up at me with a smile. "That sounds nice. We haven't done that in a while. I need about an hour to finish up, and then we can go. And after we can get manicures!"

Mom loves getting her nails done—she has ever since Aunt Nora taught her about gel manis, which stay on even though Mom deals with staples and clips and other polish-destroying supplies all day long at her job. It's her big treat to herself. Her only one, as far as I can tell.

"Where's your brother? Go ask him if he wants to go out to eat with us."

I take a shower and get dressed. Then I knock on Chance's door.

"What?" he calls out.

"It's me. See, this is how you enter a room. You knock and wait until the person says, 'Come in.' You should try it sometime."

"Got it. Come in."

I push open the door. Chance is sprawled on his bed, looking at his phone. "Mom and I are going to the diner for lunch, then we're getting our nails done. You want to go with us?"

"To get my nails done?" Chance shakes his head no. "My hands are already perfection."

"Very funny. No, I mean for lunch?"

"I can't, I have to do some stuff," he says.

"What stuff?"

"Just some stuff. I'll see you when you get back." He gives me a cheerful wave.

"Whatever," I say, closing his door.

I should have been more suspicious of Chance turning down lunch—he never misses an opportunity to eat out. And we all love the diner. We've been going there since forever, so they know our names and always give Chance an extra onion ring with his burger. But I was so busy trying to distract myself from all my stupid worries that I wasn't as focused as usual.

Knowing Chance like I do, I was a total fool for leaving him to his own devices.

14

When Mom and I get back from our outing, I head inside while she gets the mail out of our mailbox. I'm busy staring at my cute nails and trying to take the perfect photo of my hands around my cup of iced coffee when something in the hallway catches my eye.

At first I'm confused. I think there's a funny reflection from my phone or maybe a car drove by outside and flashed its lights. But then my heart jumps as I realize there's a strange person with short, bright-pink hair standing in our house.

I scream at the top of my lungs. An insane clown is in our house, waiting to kill me, just like in every scary movie ever!

It's only when the clown turns around and faces me that I realize it's my brother.

I do a double take. Chance's shaggy hair has been transformed into a super-short buzz cut, and his once-blond strands are now glow-in-the-dark neon pink. It's the brightest color hair I've seen in my whole life on anyone.

"Hey," Chance says nonchalantly, taking a sip of his orange sports drink. It clashes with his head. "Why are you screaming?"

"What happened to you?" I yell, my hands shaking. "You scared me to death! I thought you were a robber."

Mom comes in behind me. "What are you yelling about?"

Speechless, I can only point to Chance, who looks confused. It's like he's completely forgotten about his head.

Mom does a double take. Then a *triple* take. Then she gasps and puts her hand over her mouth.

"Is that a wig?" she asks quietly, her words muffled because her hand is still covering her lips.

"Yeesh, both of you, calm down, it's just hair," Chance says, rubbing his head self-consciously. "I like it."

"You look like an Easter egg," I say.

"Where is your actual hair? Please tell me that's a wig." Mom steps forward, reaching out two fingers to yank on his shorn hair.

"Ow!" Chance pulls away from her hand. "Mom, it's not a wig! This is my hair!"

"You look so weird," I say. "What happened? Did you fall into a vat of Pepto-Bismol?"

Chance ignores me.

"Did you do this here? In the bathroom?" Mom looks nervously toward the bathroom door.

"What? No way, I'm not stupid."

I snort.

Chance continues talking. "Last night when we were driving back from Spirit Night we went past Joe's Barbershop. They had a sign outside their door about a special they're running until the end of October for Breast Cancer Awareness Month."

Neither Mom nor I say anything.

"You pay them thirty dollars, and they cut your hair and dye it hot pink and donate the profits to a cancer charity. It's called Pink Hair for Hope. Get it, pink? Pink ribbon? Pink for cancer?" Chance continues. "I used some of my birthday money. Thirty dollars is a decent deal, right? For all this?" He gestures to his head happily.

Mom looks at Chance, then at me. Then back at him.

Then she starts to cry.

"All that beautiful blond hair!" she sniffles. "I can't believe you did that. You look so different." She gives him a hug and pats his head, more gently this time.

"Mom, c'mon, don't cry. Besides, I was sick of my hair. It was always in my eyes and so annoying when I'm on the field. I'm the only player on my team who has to wear a headband."

Chance often pulls his hair into a ridiculous Alexander Hamilton ponytail for soccer, but if you ask me, this is way dumber-looking.

Mom is squeezing him now, crying and laughing at the same time, and Chance is half pulling away and half hugging her back. "You didn't have to do that for me, honey," she says.

"I wanted to. It's cool. And if anyone asks me why I dyed it, I can tell them it was for you."

I haven't been able to say anything up until that moment. I was still processing how wildly different my brother looks. When we left, he was Chance. Messy, shaggy, blond hair. Jeans, tee, sneakers. A regular-looking boy in our grade. Now he stands out like a giant, flaming Q-tip.

And then it hits me—hard. Of course people will ask Chance about his hair. I mean, it's bananas looking! And people are always interested in what he does, even when it's boring. His current head situation is anything but.

"What do you think, Josephine?" Mom asks, but she doesn't wait for me to answer. "Oh, Chance, I forgot, we brought you back a burger. Are you hungry?"

"Totally. Dying your hair works up your appetite."

"It's in the kitchen. I'll keep you company. I can't believe your hair. How long did it take? Did the dye smell awful?"

I stand there for a while after they walk away, feeling all churny inside. Chance knew I wanted to keep our family's private information private. I haven't even told my best friend yet! And he totally disregarded that! I mean, I can understand his wanting to tell one or two friends, but now anyone within two-hundred yards of his head will want to know why he did what he did.

And he'll tell them everything.

Come Monday, everyone at school is going to know about Mom having cancer. And with a bright neon-pink human billboard walking the hallways, no one will think of anything else when they see me.

* * *

I spend the rest of the day furious with Chance but trying not to show it in front of Mom so she won't get angry with me. She *always* takes Chance's side. That makes me even angrier at the both of them.

Why should *I* have to tiptoe around, worrying about everyone else, while my brother goes and completely ignores my wishes? Neither of them even seem to notice I'm upset. Mom is too busy taking a bazillion photos of Chance, and then I hear her on the phone with Aunt Nora going on and on about how sweet it was of him to cut off all his hair and spend his own money.

Big whoop, I think. He probably still has the haul he made hawking those chocolate bars. Meanwhile, Mom probably wouldn't even notice if I rolled my entire body in pink glitter paint.

Sunday morning, Mom makes pancakes—another one of our food traditions—and while she cooks, I set the table and give Chance the dirtiest look I can muster. Instead of putting the fork down next to him, I shove it hard enough that it goes flying past him and onto the floor.

He bends over and picks it up. "What is your problem?" he asks me, quietly enough that Mom can't hear. "You've been acting like a jerk since I dyed my hair."

"You. You're my problem. I can't believe you did that." I gesture to his head.

Annoyed, he answers, "What do you care? It's not your hair."

"Everything you *do* is my problem," I say through gritted teeth. "Idiot."

"You're the idiot," he hisses at me, his flushed cheeks clashing with his pink head. I want to pour a bottle of maple syrup on his stupid hair.

"I told you I didn't want people to know about Mom. And then you do *that*."

"It's not about you, Josephine. I'm doing what *I* want. If you don't like it, tough."

Before I can get in another comeback, Mom brings over a stack of pancakes, and I go back to being silently mad at him.

I can't believe he's acting so clueless. Chance knows how much I hate being the focus of attention. Like when we were eight, Dad took Chance and me on a trip to visit our grandparents in Florida. Dad booked us on a super-cheap, no-frills airline, thinking he'd gotten a bargain, but when we got to the airport, we found out we had to pay extra for just about everything, like being able to sit together and checking our bags. It ended up costing a lot more money—money that Dad didn't have.

Dad flipped out. Stomping around, rolling his eyes at everyone, yelling and being rude to the counterperson. Chance and I stood there staring as Dad grumbled about what a rip-off flying was and how they charged you for everything, including the air you breathe. Finally security came over and talked quietly to Dad for a while until they were confident he wasn't dangerous.

I still remember how awful it felt to have the eyes of all the other passengers gawking at us, half pitying and half nervous, like we were some family of freaks. I wanted to melt into the floor or jump on an entirely different flight and pretend I didn't know Dad at all.

Dad may not mind causing a scene, and Chance swears he doesn't remember that incident, but in my mind, when I'm the center of attention, it's *never* for a good reason.

15

When Monday morning arrives—far too fast—I beg Mom to drive us to school so we don't have to take the bus. I know I'm only delaying the inevitable school-wide freak-out by a few minutes, but I'll take whatever I can get.

Mom has barely pulled to a full stop in front of our building before I'm out of my seat. I race across the parking lot and into the building by myself, leaving Chance as far behind me as possible. We're allowed to go upstairs to our classrooms as soon as we arrive, so I avoid lingering in the hallways like usual. Instead, I keep my head down and go straight to my math class. The room is still cool thanks to the chilly fall morning outside.

When the bell rings for the official start of class, the rest of my classmates pile in. I hear the first rush of reactions:

"Yo, did you see Chance?"

"Oh my God, how could you miss him?"

"I can't believe he did that!"

"I heard he did it because he knows someone who died last week. You know, like a tribute."

"That is so sad. Whoa. He's so strong. And brave."

"He looks hot."

I shoot the kids a look but no one notices. *Hello, seriously, Chance's twin sister over here!* I want to yell. *I can hear you!*

Of course no one asks *me* what's going on. Half the time no one even remembers Chance and I are related because we're so different. I feel like screaming, "NO ONE DIED! MY BROTHER IS JUST AN IDIOT!" at the top of my lungs, but instead I slink down lower into my seat so my head rests against the chair back.

At the end of the period, I walk into the hallway and see Makayla standing there wearing her favorite leopard-print leggings and a decidedly non-matching orange-and-pink striped shirt. She walks right up to me, touching my arm and looking worried instead of happy and Makayla-y.

This is exactly what I've been dreading. Having everyone know about Mom, things changing around me, people pitying me or being fake nice to my face. I just want things to be *normal*.

"Josephine, I saw Chance, and he told me about your mom. I am so, so, so sorry."

"Um, it's OK," I mumble.

"How come you didn't tell me? When did you find out?"

"Last week. I was going to tell you but—"

Makayla interrupts me, her expression shocked. "Wait, last week? You've known for an entire week? Why didn't you say anything? I'm supposed to be your best friend!"

"I know," I whisper, hoping she'll keep her voice down too. "I didn't want to talk about it—not with *anyone*. I just didn't. It's not you." I look down, avoiding her hurt gaze. "I have to go to class, or I'll get in trouble for being late. Can we talk later?"

Makayla doesn't respond. She looks like she's about to cry. I turn my back to her and walk off without saying anything else.

I try to ignore the whispers about Chance that I hear during my next class, but it's impossible. On my way down the hallway before third period, I pass a huge crowd of kids standing in a circle around my brother. I'm busy trying to blend in, while Chance is busy laughing at something one of them is saying. He looks totally confident in his pink hair and clashing red fleece pullover.

Diego stands right next to him. I haven't seen him in person since Autumn asked him out for me on Friday night. That feels like a million years ago. I've hardly had time to think about him—or what's going to happen at the party. Not after my stupid brother ruined the whole weekend.

As I walk by, Diego catches my eye and gives me a sympathetic-looking half smile and a subdued wave. It's not the look of a boy who thinks I'm cute and is psyched to go to a party with me.

It's a look of pity.

16

I spent all weekend stressing over going back to school and seeing everyone lose their collective minds over Chance's hair. But then I realize the worst part of the day is still to come. I can be in my own little world during class, not talking to anyone, but lunch is a different story. I'll have to see Makayla and Autumn and everyone else. I hope no one says anything about it to me. I don't think I can talk about Mom without crying, and I *so* don't want to break down in the middle of the cafeteria.

I get in line for food, so distracted that I don't even notice Chance and Autumn are standing right behind me.

"Jose, hey," Chance says, startling me out of my stare down with the turkey club sandwiches.

Autumn is touching Chance's head and smiling at him. "Hi!" she says to me, looking more serious. "Josephine, about your mom . . ."

"It's OK," I say, cutting her off and turning my head away, hoping she'll take the hint. Any lingering hope I had that the excitement over my brother would have died down is dashed.

We progress down the line of fogged-up glass partitions as we get our meals.

"Come sit with us," Autumn says to Chance. "There's plenty of room at our table."

So Chance ambles past all the other tables, kids turning to gawk at him as he passes. He doesn't even notice their stares.

Once we're settled in and eating, Emily and Makayla join us too, sitting across from me. Makayla is quieter than normal and gives me a brief smile without meeting my eyes.

Autumn turns to my brother. "I still can't get over your hair! I love it. Although it was so nice before too." She rubs the small amount of hair he has left.

Chance ducks away from her and laughs, saying, "Thanks."

I roll my eyes at both of them.

"I have a great idea," Chance says to the entire table.

Another great *idea?* I think. *One wasn't enough?*

"Actually it was Oliver's idea," he adds. "The baseball team is going to do a cancer fund-raiser."

"Oh, cool." Makayla says. She still hasn't spoken directly to me since our interrupted talk earlier that morning. I know her feelings are hurt that I didn't say anything to her, but is she actually *angry* with me about it?

"Yeah," Chance continues. "People can donate as much as they want. For every thirty dollars we raise, another player will get his hair dyed at Joe's Barbershop. They're giving all their profits to the American Cancer Society. By the end of the month, we're going to raise enough to dye the entire team."

"That is sooooo nice of you," Autumn says. "I'll totally sponsor a few haircuts."

"Thanks, Autumn," Chance replies. "That's awesome."

They stare at each other more.

Grossssssss.

I look around at the rest of the cafeteria and spot Diego sitting a few tables away, his back to us. I want to say something to him, but what? Why is everything so awkward in my life? Why am *I* so awkward? Ugh!

Just then Chance's friend Isaac Shakeel walks over and drops money into Chance's lap.

"Yo, thanks," Chance says, laughing and high-fiving him. He counts the bills. "We almost have enough for our first victim! It's gotta be Justin. He'll look insane with pink hair."

"Here, how much more do you need to get to thirty dollars?" Makayla asks, pulling her duct tape wallet, the one I made her for Christmas, out of her bag.

"We have twenty already, so just ten more," Chance replies.

She hands my brother the money. "Here. Go pink!"

I feel my nose burn, which happens when tears prickle at the back of my eyes. I rub at them with the cuff of my sweatshirt. Makayla is such a nice person. No matter what, she'll do the right thing. Meanwhile, I make one stupid, thoughtless mistake after another with the people I care about.

Makayla doesn't seem to notice I'm upset, though. She and Autumn are talking quietly about something. I can't hear what.

I glance at Chance. He looks so different that I still do a double take every time I see him to make sure it's truly my brother in there.

My life has changed as much in a week as Chance's stupid hair. On the outside, I look the same as always. But on the inside, the transformation feels as dramatic as my brother's appearance. I didn't even ask for *one* thing to change, and now it all has.

I take small, sad bites of my soggy sandwich, not really tasting it.

Just get through the rest of the day, I remind myself. *It cannot get any worse.*

17

There are few things that strike fear in the hearts of kids as much as seeing parents show up unexpectedly in the one place where they do not belong: the school building. So when I see Mom striding through the hallway right before my final period, my stomach does a little flip.

She's wearing an open beige trench coat, the belt flapping behind her, over her white shirt and red work vest with her name tag. When she sees my horrified expression, she slows down just enough to say, "I have to take care of something quickly in the front office, but don't worry, everything's fine."

"But—" I start to say.

"I'll see you later, honey. Go to class."

She hurries along, her shoes making whispers of noise, until she's swallowed up in a sea of students.

I go to art class with a lump in my stomach. We're doing a beautiful weaving project that's actually coming together for me—unlike some of my other art-related disasters. I'm pretty sure Mr. Fabel thinks I should be permanently banned from the pottery wheel. He finally gently suggested that I make a pinch pot to hold paper clips—like a kindergartener—after my third disaster in a row involving clay.

I try focusing on the feel of the wool underneath my hands and the way the colors become even more vibrant when contrasted with other colors. There's something peaceful about the experience, and I feel my body relax for the first time in forever. My classmates, as into it as I am, are quieter than normal too.

But the peace doesn't last long. Within a few minutes, the school intercom squawks on, an intermittent crackle running underneath the words: "Josephine Doukas, please report to the front office."

Every single head in the class swivels toward me. It's just as horrible as you'd imagine.

"Go ahead, Josephine," Mr. Fabel says to me as he wipes his eyeglasses off with a paint-stained cloth.

I jump up, grabbing all my stuff and shoving it into my backpack quickly. This obviously has something to do with Mom being in the building. Did she call me into the office to meet with Mrs. Hamburg even though she promised I wouldn't have to talk to the guidance counselor?

As I walk by, my classmates stare at me before focusing back on their weaving. I turn my head away so I can't see their eyes.

As soon as the art room door shuts behind me, I rush down the hallway, hoping they won't need to call my name over the intercom again. I speed up, and by the time I open the door to the main office, I'm almost running.

"Hi, I'm Josephine Doukas," I pant.

The gray-haired secretary at a desk full of bobbleheads motions me over, but before I can take a step, Mom and Chance come out of Principal Malik's office. Mom shakes Mr. Malik's hand and thanks him, then places her hand gently on my brother's shoulder, steering him forward.

"As I said, Chance may need to make arrangements to dye his hair back to a more . . . natural color unless things settle down immediately," Mr. Malik says, his voice pausing over the word *natural*. "I'm afraid this is just too distracting for his classmates."

"Let's go, Josephine," Mom says, motioning for me to join her, her lips pressed together tightly.

"You have to sign them out," the gray-haired office lady says. She reaches out and passes Mom a clipboard with a pen hanging sadly from a string and a piece of dirty masking tape.

Mom signs without speaking. Then she takes Chance and me both firmly by our arms and walks out, murmuring a curt, "Thank you."

"What's going on?" I ask. "What's wrong? And why are you making me come home early?"

"We'll discuss this in the car," Mom says, her hand gripping me tighter.

"Ow!" I protest, but Mom doesn't let up on her grip.

Chance, amazingly enough, is quiet.

As soon as we're all buckled into Mom's white hatchback, me grabbing the front seat so Chance is forced to fold himself into the back, I tap Mom on the shoulder. "What's up, Mom?"

It's Chance who speaks up. "I guess not everyone loves my hair."

"Big shocker." I turn around to look at him. "What happened?"

"Your brother has violated the dress code, I'm told." Mom shakes her head. "Unbelievable."

"It's not clothing, so why are they calling my hair a dress-code violation anyway?" Chance sits back, arms folded across his chest.

"What do you mean?" I ask. "And why did I have to miss art class for this?" I turn to Mom, then whip around to Chance. "I told you this was a stupid idea!"

"Josephine, leave your brother alone. He's had a bad enough day."

I can't believe what I'm hearing. Seriously? Chance is having a bad day? How can she not see that my day was infinitely worse?

"Please, like I haven't?" I say. "Everyone's talking about us and staring at us!"

"No one is staring at *you*, Jose," Chance says. "No one even notices you."

All three of us freeze.

I feel like crying.

"Excuse me for not being desperate for attention," I snap, opening and shutting the glove compartment over and over.

"You're going to break that," Mom says, leaning over and swatting my hand away. "And I don't want to pay to fix it."

"Fine," I say angrily, sitting back. "Glad you're more worried about the car than about your own daughter!"

Mom shoots a glance at me before turning back to the road. "Josephine, please, I can't deal with your attitude right now. What Chance and I were *trying* to explain is that Mr. Malik said Chance's hair is causing so much commotion during class that students aren't paying attention. He gave Chance a warning to keep things from getting out of hand. If things don't change, he'll have to dye his hair back, or Mr. Malik may have to take further action."

"Further action like what?" I ask, confused. "Not to defend Captain Stupid back there, but half the school has dyed streaks and bleached tips and stuff in their hair. Kindergarteners get hair streaks!"

"I don't want to discuss it," Mom says, pulling out of the parking lot. But she goes on like she can't help herself. "I normally take your school's side on things, but this makes me extremely angry! It's hair. It's hardly offensive!"

"I guess I'm on Mr. Malik's bad side already because of the food fight," Chance says, looking sheepish. "And the chocolate bar thing. And the—"

Mom grips the steering wheel tighter. "Chance, I don't care about all those things. What you did this time was wonderful, and I'm proud of you."

"Thanks, Mom," Chance says.

"But you're still going to have to stop talking over teachers or causing any distractions during class," she adds. "Otherwise you're dyeing your hair back."

"What about my fund-raiser?" Chance whines.

Mom turns around to stare at him. "What fund-raiser?" she asks, jerking the wheel so we lurch back into our lane.

"Mom, watch the road!" I shriek.

"The whole baseball team is raising money to dye their hair like me. The more money we get, the more of us will do it."

Mom rubs the side of her head with the heel of her hand like she has a headache, taking a deep breath. Through pressed lips, she says, "You didn't mention that back in our meeting."

Chance shrugs. "I didn't think that would be smart. I doubt Mr. Malik knows anything about it."

"Yet," I mutter.

"Maybe if we just got streaks instead—" Chance begins.

Mom cuts him off. "I don't see how getting more people involved is a good idea right now. You'll have to thank your teammates for their kindness but ask them to find another way to support cancer research. A fund-raiser is still a wonderful idea. Why don't you have a bake sale?"

Chance nods glumly.

"I still don't understand why I had to get pulled out of class for this. I'm not the one causing a 'commotion,'" I say to Mom, putting air quotes around *commotion*.

"You had less than fifteen minutes left in your day, Josephine. I didn't think you'd mind getting out of school early or getting a ride home instead of taking the bus. After all, you were so eager to have me drive you this morning."

I roll my eyes. "Mom, I do mind! I was having a good time weaving! Not that anyone cares what I want."

"Yes, that's right, no one cares," Mom says sarcastically. "I'm a monster."

"It's always all about him!"

Mom grips the steering wheel even tighter. "That is not true."

Ignoring her, I turn to yell over my shoulder at Chance. "I told you the whole idea was idiotic!"

Mom turns to me, furious. "And I *told you* to leave him alone!"

"Whatever! Take his side like you always do!"

"What are you talking about?" she says, her voice even angrier. "There are no sides here. We're a family."

I make a gagging noise, then roll down the window and stick my head out so I can pretend not to hear either one of them. The air feels cool against my face, which has gotten hot from the warm air in the car and from arguing with my brother. We ride the rest of the way home in silence.

When we get home, Mom stops me before I go into my room.

"I don't feel like talking right now," I tell her, looking down at my feet.

"I don't care, Josephine. I'm not asking—I'm telling. Sit down." Her lips are pinched tightly together, making her look mean.

"Fine. What?"

She takes a seat on the couch, but I stay standing.

"You seem quite upset," Mom says, speaking slowly and evenly. I hate when she talks to me like I'm a baby.

"I'm not upset."

"It's understandable if you're angry."

This time, I don't say anything. I'm too furious to speak.

She continues, "I know thinking about my surgery is scary. I'm upset too. So is your brother. It's normal to be frightened."

I focus in on what she's saying about Chance, ignoring the rest of it. "What are you talking about? He doesn't even seem sad, Mom. He's having fun dyeing his hair and making a big deal out of everything and getting all the attention. I told him I didn't want everyone to know about you!"

Mom's eyes open wider. "Honey, why not?"

I don't answer. I'm worried if I start talking, it will all come flying out of me, and I won't be able to stop until I've made Mom feel worse than I do.

Everything bad runs through my mind. How different things are for us compared to my friends. Dad rarely comes to our school events. Most of my friends don't even have divorced parents, and even if they do, their dads don't live two hours away. And now I have a sick mom, and everyone I know is giving me these stupid, pitying looks.

Instead of saying any of that, I reply, "I just didn't want my business shared with everyone, OK? Why can't Chance respect that?"

"Because Chance has a different way of coping with things than you do. He always has."

I shake my head. I knew Mom wouldn't get it. Any time Chance and I disagree, Mom always takes his side. It's so unfair. I know Chance is sad about Mom having cancer, but he isn't angry about it. He's not mad at anyone. He's still as happy as ever. And that makes me even more furious.

"Well I wish his way didn't constantly affect me. You have no idea what it's like having someone around all the time, bothering you, always needing to be the center of attention, and ruining everything! Are we done now? Can I go?"

I don't wait to see Mom's hurt expression before I storm off to my room and slam my door shut. Then I burst into tears, feeling overwhelmed with shame and anger, the two emotions so mixed up inside me that I'm not sure I'll ever feel normal again.

18

Mom comes into my room later without knocking. "I don't want to talk," I say.

"Fine. Don't talk. But you can listen. I know you're having a hard time, but so are the rest of us. Try remembering that and being less rude." Before I can reply, she shuts my door with more force than necessary.

She leaves me alone after that, and lets Chance come get me when it's time for dinner. I sit quietly during the meal as she and Chance talk about whatever.

I tune them out. I have nothing to say to either of them, and they don't seem to notice—or care—that I'm completely silent.

Then I get a brilliant idea. You know that song from *Hamilton*? "Talk less. Smile more. Don't let them know what you're against or what you're for."

At school, the kids who get the most attention are the ones who get into trouble with teachers or cause drama with classmates. People talk about them. People watch them. If I don't want to be the center of attention, I need to start acting like everything is OK and blend in. If I do that, no one will bug me or ask me to talk about things or talk about me when I'm not around.

It will all be back to normal. Or normal-ish.

Makayla texts me during dinner, asking why they called my name at school, but thanks to the no-phones-at-the-table rule I have an excuse not to reply right away. Instead I mentally plan my reply to her, trying to make everything sound funny instead of horrible.

Tip: It's easier to lie in text than face-to-face.

Oh HAHA guess what? My mom had to come to talk about Chance's hair! I text once I'm back in my room.

Really? That's so funny!!!!

IKR!

So now what?

Oh nothing, they just wanted Mom to come in to DISCUSS things. So he would stop distracting everyone. No big deal.

Cool

Pretending I was OK was easier than I thought. I even worked my nerve up to text: **Sorry that I was weird about stuff**

♥U she texts back.

Victory! I hope that cleared the air.

At school the next day, two different people try to talk to me about Chance and his drama. Sara Glassman attempts to corner me at my locker, and even though I just have study hall next, I tell her, "I'm soooo busy, I have to finish my lab, or I'll be in trouble, sorry!" and race off.

With Owen Southard, who hasn't talked to me in like, three years, I just say, "Oh, you know Chance, ha ha."

So far I'm proving to be a better actress than I thought. The only time I've acted before was the summer I went to our local theater camp. I was a member of the chorus in *Fiddler on the Roof,* but I still remember the director telling the older kids that: "Acting means you have to believe what you're saying, or at least believe that your character believes it."

And now, here I am doing an award-winning job pretending things are normal. At least on the outside.

* * *

Each morning after that, I tear another page off my one-a-day *Dr. Who* calendar and watch as we draw nearer and closer to October seventh—the day of Mom's surgery.

Every day closer I get more anxious. It feels like something is squeezing tighter and tighter around my throat. Acting like I'm fine around Makayla and the rest of the girls gets harder and harder. Not to mention I haven't even spoken to Diego beyond an occasional "Hey" in the hallways. He hasn't been to our house to visit Chance at all, and I hope that isn't because he's avoiding me.

Ten days left. The start of our last full normal week together.

Nine days left. I get a B+ back on the math test I was sure I bombed. That's good.

Eight days left. I beat an eighth grader named Bettina Dereven in chess. Makayla says it's the best playing I'd ever done.

Seven days left. One week to go.

Six days left. I trip in my flip-flops and skin my knee. It hurts more than it should.

Five days left. It's time for First Friday. It takes place in the center of our town—you guessed it, every first Friday—and they keep the shops and restaurants open late, and food trucks serve tacos and barbeque and stuff. The best part is the cupcake truck. Mom takes Chance and me, and we all walk around. It's a good place to not have to talk, because it's busy and they have a jazz trio playing in the village parking lot. But even so, I feel sad being there, like what if something happens to Mom while she's in the hospital and this is the very last First Friday the three of us will ever have?

I know Mom is worried too, even though she keeps acting like she's not. It's obvious from the tension on her face and the way she hasn't smiled for real in what feels like forever. I wish I could say something to her so she wouldn't feel so alone, but I'm not sure how to bring it up and what to say, so instead, I do nothing.

I end up giving Chance half of my red-velvet cupcake because I lose my appetite.

Four days left. Chance's friend Isaac sleeps over.

Three days left. Chance has an away game, so while he gets a ride with Isaac's family, I stay home with Mom and do homework. She cooks two lasagnas, one to eat and one to freeze so we can reheat it later.

When she's in the hospital.

Two days left. The start of Mom's surgery week.

One.

The night before Mom's operation, Chance and I offer to make dinner. He's been quieter than normal the past few days, but while we're cooking, he's more silent than I've seen him in, like, the entire time we've been alive.

When dinner is ready, we all sit at the table and pick at our food, pushing the chicken and rice around on our plates, no one talking much. Mom goes over all the details for the next day and makes it clear that she expects us to go to school in the morning, rather than go to the hospital where we'll have nothing to do but sit and worry. Dad will be waiting for us when we get home from school, and then he'll drive us to the hospital in the evening so we can visit Mom. She's gone over the details with us a bunch of times and now she writes it up and puts all the information on the fridge, even though she doesn't need to.

It's impossible to forget what's happening.

Chance asks to be excused from dinner early, claiming that he has a science test to study for, but I think he's just too bummed to be around Mom.

Mom and I do the dishes without him. We're standing side by side, me washing, the suds warm and soft against my hands, and Mom drying the plates with her old red-and-white striped dish towel. Then, out of the blue, she takes a big, deep breath and says, "If something were to happen to me, you'd be OK."

I watch as a bubble in the sink grows bigger, reflecting a rainbow, before popping. It looks like my heart feels.

My voice breaking, I say, "Mom, what are you talking about? You said nothing bad is going to happen!"

"Josephine, honey, I hope and pray that I'll be around for a long time. But you're worried. I can see that. And I want you to know, there are a lot of people in the world besides me who care about you. Aunt Nora. Your father. Grandma Clara. Your brother."

"Mom." I try to say something, but I start sobbing. Before I know it, I'm crying so hard I can't see the dishes.

Mom turns off the water and gives me a big hug, grabbing me and rocking back and forth like I'm a baby.

"I'm getting you all soapy," I say, my face muffled up against her black sweatshirt. I try to pull away, but she smushes me up against her some more.

"I don't care," she says. "This is going in the wash tonight anyway."

I'm still crying as I tell her, "I've been so awful to everyone lately. If you die I'll hate myself forever."

There's silence as my comment registers with both of us.

I can't believe I said it out loud.

Mom pulls back so she can look me in the eyes. "I am not going to die."

I sniffle. "I'm so sorry about everything."

"You have nothing to apologize for, Josephine. Cancer is nobody's fault. I wish this wasn't happening to any of us, but no one is to blame for this. It's just bad luck." Mom squeezes me again.

"But I've been so mean. To you and to Chance. I was terrible to him the day he got into trouble at school. And afterward. And I still haven't apologized."

Mom studies me carefully. "Chance knows you love him. And so do I."

"I've been making things worse for you instead of better," I go on, sobbing, as if she hasn't spoken. "It's like I can't even remember how to be nice anymore."

Mom smiles at that. "Of course you can. You're being nice right now. Besides, I don't expect you to make things better for me. I'm the adult here, not you."

I shrug. "I know, Mom, but still!"

"You're twelve. You shouldn't have to worry about me or take care of me. Or Chance, for that matter."

"But if I don't, who will?"

Mom shakes her head. "I'm the grown-up here. I can take care of myself, and I can take care of you and your brother too. That's *my* job, not yours."

I'm not sure I believe her. It seems like Mom has too many jobs already, but when I take a breath, I feel lighter than I have in days. As if the squeezing of my throat loosened slightly. That night, when I go to bed, I set my alarm for extra early so I can spend time with Mom before she leaves for the hospital. That way she can leave knowing how much I love her.

19

Mom's friend Mrs. Toyoshima comes by the next morning to pick Mom up and bring her to the hospital. They'll head out right after we leave for school. Mrs. Toyoshima gives me and Chance a quick but friendly greeting and then gives Mom a hug as Chance and I stand there awkwardly watching.

Mrs. Toyoshima tells us about how she has all these friends who are breast cancer survivors and are "completely cured." Chance and I nod. Then she and Mom go get Mom's bag while Chance and I finish getting ready.

"You hungry?" Chance asks, taking a box of waffles out of the freezer. The roots of his hair are just starting to show—you can see a tiny bit of blond hair fighting to peek out from the pink.

"I'm not at all hungry," I reply.

"Me either." He takes four waffles out of the box and sticks them into the toaster oven. Four waffles for Chance is a light snack. One time I saw him eat an entire box.

"Are you glad that Dad's coming?" he asks as the toaster glows brightly behind him.

"Kind of. Are you?"

Chance shakes his head. "I mean, it's weird, him staying here again. It's not his house anymore, you know?"

I shrug. We haven't seen Dad in a while, so I'm glad he's coming to be with us. Even if it is for an awful reason.

"Don't miss the bus!" Mom yells from down the hall. "Let me come say goodbye."

Then she's there, hugging us.

"Bye, Mom," I say, starting to cry into her shoulder.

Then Chance starts crying too.

Mom stands there for a minute, squeezing us both and saying, "Shhhh. Don't worry. I promise, it's going to be fine."

"OK." I sniffle, pulling back.

Then it's time. Mom waves goodbye and tries to act cheerful, even though none of us are buying it.

At school, I try to push thoughts of Mom aside so I can have a regular, normal day. I sit with Makayla and the rest of the girls at lunch, which I skipped the day before to hide out in the library. I haven't told anyone that Mom is in the hospital at this very moment, not even Makayla, so no one asks me how I'm doing or anything. Instead they discuss their outfits for Autumn's party on Saturday, and how we're all going to spend the afternoon getting ready together and how cool it is that Autumn's family has a chef, who's going to make us something special for lunch.

"My mom is going to get someone to come in and give us manis too," Autumn adds.

Talk less. Smile more. Don't let them know what you're against or what you're for.

I laugh along with them, making jokes about the boys and how I can't believe Autumn likes my brother and about how cute Diego is. But part of me feels like I'm sitting ten tables over, observing an alien species who care about entirely different things than I do.

I just wish the day would end already so I can visit Mom.

After my last class, I get my phone from my locker and turn it back on. We aren't allowed to have our phones on us during school hours. There's a message from Dad that sounds like he's far away, talking on a speakerphone.

"Hi, Josephine! It's me. It's two o'clock, and I'm stuck in traffic leaving Philadelphia. I'll be at the house a little later than we'd planned, OK? See you soon! Love you!"

Two o'clock? I think. How is he just leaving Philadelphia? Even without traffic, it takes two and a half hours to get from his apartment to Croton. He told us—and Mom!—that he'd be at our house by early afternoon, before we got home from school. He *promised*. Mom even FedExed him a copy of the house keys the week before so he'd be able to let himself in.

I run to make the bus, and as soon as I get on, I text Chance two rows back to tell him:

Dad isn't at the house yet

He writes back: Where is he?

Stuck in traffic

WHATEVER

So we come home to an empty house, just like usual. Except this time the quiet is quieter than normal. It's strange and sad. Permanent. I know Mom won't be walking in the door that night to have dinner with us.

"Maybe we can get a ride to the hospital with someone else," Chance says as we dump our bags on the floor and kick off our shoes.

"Dad's on his way. He *said* he's coming," I snap at him. I don't want to admit it, but I desperately wish Dad would hurry up too. Visiting hours last until seven-thirty, but I want to be there, like, now.

Otherwise Mom will be all alone when she needs us the most. I can't bear the thought.

"Like, on his way as in he's a half a mile from here, or on his way as in he's just leaving his house in Philadelphia?" Chance sounds upset.

"He left the message at two, and said he was in traffic in Philadelphia."

Chance presses his lips together, looking furious. "Two? Why didn't he leave earlier than two?"

"Chance, I don't know!" I yell. "Why don't you call him and ask?"

Chance doesn't respond. He just walks away from me silently.

I sit down with my notebook at the kitchen table and try to get some homework done while I wait, but I can't stop looking up at the wall clock. Upon closer inspection it looks dingy and has a splatter of sauce on it.

Where is Dad? I think.

Five minutes later, Chance comes back in, looking angrier than I've seen him in forever. "I just called Dad, and he said it's going to be 'a while.'"

"What? How is that possible?" I look at the clock again. It's already half past four. "Could we take a cab?" I ask.

Chance shakes his head. "We don't have the money for that. It's, like, a twenty-minute ride at least. I'd ask Diego, but I know his parents won't be home until later, and Mrs. Toyoshima is at work." He looks at me, helplessly. "Jose, what do we do?"

Instead of answering him, I pull out my cell phone. I call Makayla's house number instead of her cell. After two rings, her mom picks up.

"Hi, Josephine. How are you, honey?"

I burst into tears. "Mrs. Kaiser, Chance and I need help."

Less than fifteen minutes later, Mrs. Kaiser is pulling up to our front door in her shiny black car, her face all worried. She comes out of the car to give me a hug, her puffy vest pressing reassuringly against my cheek. Chance and I get into the back seat, and he slams the door shut behind him.

"Thank you for coming to get us," I say quietly. I've stopped crying for now, but I'm close to starting up again. "Is Makayla at home?"

Mrs. Kaiser catches my eye in the rearview mirror. "I wasn't sure if you wanted company tonight, so she stayed home. Would you like me to turn on the radio? Or no?"

Chance and I both shrug at the same time. Neither of us speak while Mrs. Kaiser drives us to the hospital and finds a parking spot in the dark garage.

When we get out of the car, I shiver in my short-sleeved T-shirt and leggings. The once-warm day is now noticeably cooler, like fall has arrived in the span of a few hours.

A tiny old woman sitting at the visitors' desk gives us directions, and we take the elevator to the fifth floor, where Mom's room is located. I try not to stare into any of the open rooms as the three of us walk silently down the endlessly long hallway, but I can't help it. There are all sorts of people in them—some look really old, but a lot aren't. Every single person looks sick, though. In one room, the woman lying in the bed with a tube in her nose catches my eye and smiles at me. I avert my eyes quickly, embarrassed to be caught staring.

"Mom's room is next," Chance says, scanning the numbers on the wall.

I hang back, nervous to see her, but Chance barges right in, not waiting to see if I'm behind him or not. Mrs. Kaiser waits in the hallway as I follow my brother.

Mom is sitting up in bed, bandages peeking out from above her hospital gown. Her face looks pale, and there's a tube running from her arm to a big pouch of what looks like water hanging on a metal rod next to her.

She smiles at us sleepily as Chance and I come toward the side of her bed.

"Hi, Mom," I say, almost shy with her.

"Hi," she replies, her voice quiet and scratchy. "How are you?"

"How are *you*?" Chance asks, sitting down in a chair next to her.

"I'm doing OK. I'm tired, but I feel better than I thought I would."

"What did the doctor say? Do you know when you'll be coming home?" I ask, biting my nail and then realizing I still have old nail polish on my fingers. I wonder if the polish has flaked off and is now stuck in my teeth.

"I'll find out tomorrow. But they said the procedure went well, and now I'm supposed to rest. They think I'll be discharged on Friday."

"Does it hurt?" Chance asks quietly.

Mom moves her hand slowly across the blanket on her lap. "Not too much. Mostly I'm sleepy from all the medicine they gave me, and the nurses keep waking me up to see how I'm feeling, so it's hard to rest."

I'm quiet. I don't know what to say. Mom's body seems smaller than normal. Softer. It's weird. I mean, it is *Mom*. But there in the hospital I can't imagine talking to her about anything regular, so I stay silent.

"Where's your father?" Mom asks, looking behind us at the empty doorway.

"He didn't show up," Chance says angrily.

"What?" Mom's sleepy eyes flicker, her face confused.

"Chance, SHUT UP," I hiss. "Mom, it's totally fine! Dad was running late so Makayla's mom gave us a ride. But he's on his way."

Just then Mrs. Kaiser sticks her head into the room, probably because she heard us talking about her. "May I come in?"

Mom struggles to sit up higher. "Hello, Tracy. Yes, you can come in."

"Are you sure?" Mrs. Kaiser asks. "I don't want to interrupt."

"Oh, it's fine. This is a surprise," Mom says. "I hear you drove Chance and Josephine over?"

"It's not a problem," Mrs. Kaiser says. "Anytime. I'm happy to help however I can. We all are."

Mom blinks a bunch, looking like she's going to cry. "Josephine, Chance, maybe you could go down to the cafeteria and get a ginger ale for me," she says. "I'm thirsty."

She looks around, I guess for her purse, but Mrs. Kaiser reaches into her wallet and hands us a credit card. "If you're hungry, get yourselves something to eat too. I'm in no hurry."

The two of us shuffle out of the room and make the long walk back to the elevators, still not talking. It's not until we're pushing open the door to the cafeteria that Chance speaks. "I'll find a table. Get me some food, OK?"

I nod and get in line with a tray, grabbing a yogurt and a banana for myself and a ginger ale for Mom. There's hardly any other food left except for a piece of meatloaf under a bright orange heat lamp and a sad, wilted salad with a lone crouton sitting on top. I take them both for Chance, even though the meatloaf smells weird.

I pay and look around for my brother, who isn't hard to spot. His hair is a beacon from across the cafeteria.

We sit together, and he grunts, "Thank you," before devouring his entire slice of meatloaf. Yuck.

"Let's go up," he says, still chewing his last bite. "We can give Mom her soda."

Makayla's mom is outside Mom's room waiting for us. "Your father is inside," she says, gesturing to Mom's room. "So I'll get going." She gives me a hug and pats Chance on the shoulder, then walks away.

Mom looks half asleep, and Dad is standing by the side of her bed, bouncing awkwardly on the balls of his feet. He's wearing a gray fedora with a black band around the rim and a white linen short-sleeved shirt. He hasn't shaved, so he has the faint beginning of a beard. If he was holding a drink in a coconut with a tiny umbrella in it, he'd look like he was on a tropical vacation.

"Hey, kids!" Dad says cheerfully, reaching for us for a hug. Chance shrinks back, but I let Dad hug me. He feels strong and solid and smells clean and soapy. It blocks the hospital smell in my nose for a too-brief instant.

"Sorry I'm late," he continues. "The traffic was unbelievable! Then I had to drop my bag off at the house."

"Mom's house, you mean," Chance mutters, his face furious.

Dad ignores that. "You guys look great! Chance, I think you've gotten two inches taller since last month. What's with the hair?"

No one says anything. Chance deliberately keeps his face turned away from Dad.

"It's a long story, Dad," I finally say when it's clear Chance isn't going to speak.

Before the awkwardness can continue any longer, a young-looking nurse comes in wearing a bright-green uniform and matching bright-green nail polish. She takes out an electric thermometer and puts it in Mom's mouth.

Dad pats Mom on the leg. "You look good, Allison," he says.

Mom gives him a look as the nurse takes her temperature, then wraps a cuff around her arm to take her blood pressure.

"I should have known you'd be late," Mom says tiredly.

Dad shrugs and looks down at the floor. "Look, I'm sorry, but I'm here now."

"Visiting time is almost up," the nurse says to Dad, not smiling.

"Thank you," he replies, giving her his big Dad I'll-win-you-over-yet grin. It almost always works. "We'll be leaving soon."

Just then his cell phone rings. "I'll wait outside while you two say goodbye to your mom."

As the nurse takes a stethoscope to Mom's chest, Mom says, "You two should go home and get your homework done. You can call me tomorrow in the morning before school, if you'd like. I'll be here."

We each give Mom a peck on her cheek, careful not to touch her bandages and tubes. "I love you," she says to each of us. "See you soon."

In the hallway, Dad is talking on his phone. "I'll call you later, baby," he says, then slips his phone back into his shirt pocket.

"Is that Linda?" I ask him. Linda is Dad's girlfriend.

"No. Actually, I've been meaning to tell you, Linda and I broke up," Dad says, looking sheepish.

Chance and I look at each other. Linda was Dad's third girlfriend since the divorce. Now it looks like he's on to his fourth. In four years! Mom hasn't had a single boyfriend in all that time. As far as I know, she's only been on one date, with a sales rep she met when he tried to get her store to stock his company's brand of recycled printer paper.

"So who was that on the phone?" Chance crosses his arms over his chest.

"A friend. You'll meet her next time you visit, OK? How's your mom?"

Neither Chance nor I say anything. I can tell what my brother is thinking, since I'm thinking the same thing: *Why is Dad even on the phone with this latest girlfriend anyway? He couldn't wait a few minutes?*

The idea of Dad staying with us seemed fun at first, or at least like a small, bright spot in a dark day, but now that he's here, he seems out of place. I wish Mom was the one coming home with us. Instead we walk quietly down the hallway, getting farther and farther away, while Mom lies alone in her room.

20

As we drive home from the hospital, Makayla texts me to ask how Mom is doing. **OK**, I write back.

I'm glad.

Me too.

I smile a little at that but don't respond, and Makayla doesn't say anything else. Maybe she's waiting for me to tell her more, but I'm too wiped out to even move a finger.

When we get back to the house, I go into my bedroom, yell good night to Dad and Chance, throw myself into bed, and sleep. I don't move until my alarm wakes me up the next morning. When I finally drag myself out of bed, still groggy and exhausted, Dad is still asleep on the couch. He wakes up when he hears me and comes into the kitchen as I'm eating a bowl of cereal, his hair disheveled.

"Does your mom still get the newspaper delivered?" he asks, scooping coffee grinds into the coffee machine.

I shake my head. "She doesn't have time to read it."

"So, any plans for today?" Dad asks.

"Um, you mean other than school?"

He laughs. "Oh yeah, forgot about that. I'm so used to seeing you on your days off."

I roll my eyes. "Great, Dad. Chance should get up," I remind him. "Otherwise he'll miss the bus."

"On it," Dad replies, strolling away with a cheerful whistle.

I go take a shower, leaving Dad to wake Chance up. It so isn't my problem. Unlike my brother, I didn't hit the snooze button this morning, so I have time to call Mom at the hospital before we leave for school. She picks up right away.

"Mom. It's me."

"Hi, honey. What time is it?" She sounds more alert than she did the night before.

"Did I wake you? I wanted to call before I had to go to school."

"Oh no, you didn't wake me. They come around all the time to take your temperature and blood pressure here, so I've been up for a while."

"Are you feeling OK?" I ask.

"Surprisingly, yes," she answers. "And my doctor already came by to tell me they'll discharge me tomorrow. Isn't that great?"

"Really? Yay!" I smile from ear to ear. That's a huge relief. They wouldn't send her home if anything was wrong.

"She said it would be sometime midmorning," she continues. "Aunt Nora is going to come to the hospital to pick me up, so we should be home before you and your brother get back from school."

"Are you sure you'll be back by then?" I ask. I don't want to be let down again, although it's not like Mom to do that.

"I'm positive! I'm feeling like my regular self. How's Chance?"

I don't want to tell Mom how mad Chance is at Dad. She'll just try to smooth things over, and I don't think she should be worrying about anyone but herself right now.

"He's fine. Getting ready for school. He'll be glad to know you're coming home tomorrow too."

"Give him a hug for me. Let me speak to your father for a minute, please. I can't wait to see you!"

I find Dad and hand him my cell phone. He and Mom talk for a minute or two with Dad mostly saying, "Uh-huh" and "OK." When the call is over, he gives me back my phone. "Sounds like your mom is doing well."

"She'll be home tomorrow."

Dad nods. "Right. Guess I'll head out after you guys go to school tomorrow then. I've got those two gigs Friday night. But if you want me to stay for any reason . . ."

He pauses for a minute, looking at me. Does he want me to ask him to stay? Or give him permission to go?

I shake my head. "It's fine. Mom and Aunt Nora will be here when we get home from school."

He looks relieved, and I wonder if it has to do with making his shows or Mom coming home.

I wish it wasn't so hard to tell.

* * *

At lunchtime I get to the cafeteria earlier than anyone else, so I sit down, take *Mad Magazine* and my lunch out of my backpack, and start eating. Then Emily comes and sits down across from me.

"Josephine, guess what?" she said brightly.

"Uh, what?" I say.

"I had the coolest idea. I want to get a pink streak in my hair!" Emily points to an area toward the front of her head. "Like, this much."

"Oh," I say. "That sounds cool."

"What does?" Anna asks, sitting down next to Emily at our table.

"I want to get a pink streak right here." Emily pulls at her long, sideswept bangs and holds her hair out for Anna to examine.

"Ooh, that would look so pretty with your hair!" Anna says excitedly.

"What would?" Makayla asks, plopping down her tray of mozzarella sticks. She gives my hand a little squeeze before taking a bite of her food.

"A pink streak in my hair," Emily says again. "You know, like, for Chance's charity? Plus it would look so cute."

"I'll do it too," Makayla says, mid-chew. "I'm getting bored of my hair anyway, and I need a change."

Autumn sits down with us. "What's up, girlies?"

"Makayla and I want pink streaks in our hair," Emily explains. "Inspired by Chance's fund-raiser. And, Jo, you too, of course. I mean, she's your mom too, and . . ."

"Chance will be psyched," I tell her, unsure of what else to say. They're being so nice that I don't have it in me to tell them Chance is in trouble for having pink hair and they probably shouldn't be doing any dyeing any time soon.

"Me too!" Anna jumps in.

"That's such a good idea," Autumn says. "Maybe we can get a stylist to come over on Saturday, and we can all do it for my party?" She looks at me. "We'll still donate money to Chance for charity, no matter where we do it."

Makayla actually bounces in her seat. "That would be awesome!"

"I'll ask my mom's assistant, and she can help us figure it out," Autumn says. "Do you want pink too, Josephine?"

I shrug. Somehow I don't think a second Doukas with pink hair is such a good idea, but I don't want to spoil things.

By now Noah has joined us too, and he interrupts our discussion. "Didn't you hear?" he says. "The principal is going to make Chance dye his hair back. And ban any more hair dyeing."

"Wait, what?" I say. "Who told you?"

"Oliver had to get his braces tightened so he came to school late. He overheard the principal talking to the receptionist about the dress code when he went to get a late pass."

"That's so stupid," I say, annoyed on my brother's behalf. "It's just hair. There are more important things in the world than a stupid dress code."

"Maybe Oliver misheard?" Autumn bites her lip. "I didn't even know we even had a dress code."

"He said that Mr. Malik is planning on making copies to distribute to everyone in the building," Noah says.

I look around for Chance. I hope it isn't true. He'll be so bummed!

But sure enough, during last period, each of the teachers hands out copies of a booklet that says WESTCHESTER NORTH MIDDLE SCHOOL DRESS CODE on the front. There's a single piece of paper stapled to it with two dotted lines for where we're supposed to sign it and have a parent sign it too, stating that we understand the rules and will comply with them.

What a joke!

People are totally laughing over the rules during our entire bus ride home. One part says we must wear shorts that reach to our fingertips—whatever that means—and all sorts of other stuff that makes no sense, like: "Clothes may not be inside out or backward, and must stay up/on independently." There's also a whole section on no hats, and "appropriate" hairstyles.

I text Chance, who's sitting two rows behind me:

Sorry about the hair

Sux

Totally.

Then he pops forward and lurches down next to me. I take out my earphones and look at him expectantly. "Yes?"

For a long time he just sits there, snapping a rubber band on his wrist and not saying anything.

"It was a dumb idea," Chance finally says, rubbing at his hair. "I just wanted to do something nice for Mom. But now I'm in trouble *again*, and you're mad at me *again*."

"Chance," I say, feeling tears prick at the back of my eyelids, "it was nice. Mom really appreciated it. And I'm not mad at you."

"Yes, you are." He snaps his rubber band again. "You're *always* mad at me."

"I'm not mad. I'm happy, because you made Mom super happy."

Chance gives me a look.

My voice quavers. "Besides, I was more scared than mad. I wanted you to pretend everything was OK." I give him a smile. "Seriously, you're brave to do that to your head. Even if you look crazy. I'd be too chicken. I'm too chicken to do a lot of things that you do."

Chance looks at me and shakes his head. "No, you're not. You did the high dive at the pool an entire summer before I got my nerve up to try."

"Yeah, but otherwise I'm a total wuss compared to you. Mr. Malik is a jerk for making you dye your hair back. He has no taste."

"I'm pretty sure this isn't a fashion-based decision, Jose," Chance says, a little more cheerfully, but then his face falls. "People keep giving me money so that everyone on the baseball team can get their hair dyed. I thought Mr. Malik was going to let it go, but we were all talking about it in computer science, and Owen found this app where you can upload your photo and add funny hair to your profile, and Mr. Rushton got mad and made me go to Mr. Malik's office. *Again.* I guess I'll have to give all the money back now."

I shake my head at him. I didn't realize he was still squirreling money away. "Chance! You told Mom weeks ago that you weren't going to do the fund-raiser."

"No, I didn't."

"Yes you did. I was right there. She said you couldn't draw more attention to yourself and should do a bake sale instead. Remember?"

"I remember that I never said the words, 'I'll stop.' I just nodded when she told me to."

"So? Since when is nodding yes not an actual yes?"

Chance nods at me with a big smirk on his face.

"Chance!" I yell. "Why does everything you do involve so much trouble?"

He doesn't even have the grace to look guilty. So typical!

"I really was going to drop the idea," he says, "but then everyone kept throwing more money at me. There are already like ten guys ready to go get their hair dyed pink after our soccer game a week from Sunday. I didn't want to call the whole thing off! What's the fun in that?"

I roll my eyes at him. "The fun is in not getting detention for the rest of the year. Now what? No one is going to want to get their hair dyed if they're going to get into major trouble for it."

"I could just give the money directly to a cancer charity," Chance says, speaking slowly. It's clear from his tone how bad that idea sounds to him. "I mean, it is a good cause. I doubt people would mind if I did that."

"You could," I agree. "But I'm guessing from your voice that you don't want to."

"I mean, it's not a bad thing. . . . It's just that it would have been really awesome to see an entire field of players all with hair like this." He points to his head. "But I'm sure Coach Mike will shut that down."

I stop listening because I've suddenly been struck by a crazy idea. The sort of idea that Chance has all the time and I always talk him out of because it's stupid and will undoubtedly get him into massive trouble.

But in that moment, it seems like exactly the right thing to do.

21

The next morning we set our plan in motion. We have a limited time frame to work with. Everything needs to be taken care of between when Dad leaves and Mom gets home with Aunt Nora.

"Dad," I say, as he sits across from me, drinking his coffee and looking at something on his phone. "When are you leaving to drive back home?"

"I haven't gotten that far, Josephine. I guess after you go to school?"

"Mom told you that school has a delayed opening today, right? Because of the superintendent's meeting?"

Dad looks confused. "The what?"

"They have these morning meetings twice a year where school opens late," I lie. "Our bus won't be picking us up until eleven-thirty."

"I don't remember your mom saying anything about it."

I look at him innocently. "She probably forgot. What with everything, you know?"

I know Dad will believe me. I'm a fantastic liar, which no one except Chance realizes. It's like my secret super-power. I rarely need to use it, but when I do . . . kapow! *Meet SuperLiar!*

Chance comes into the kitchen, perfectly timed to catch the end of our conversation. "Yeah, that's right, Dad. No school until later," he says, trying to seem subtle.

Chance is an atrocious liar, which is a shame consider-ing how often he needs to get out of stupid situations of his own making. He raises his eyebrows as he talks, just like he always does when he's not telling the truth.

I look away, trying not to giggle.

"You probably have to get on the road, right?" I con-tinue. "Don't worry if you leave before our bus comes, Dad. We'll be fine." I can't believe we're about to get away with it. This is way easier than I expected!

Chance nods along with me, his head bobbing.

"Oh, and you're supposed to sign this." I slide the dress code form across the table to Dad. "It just shows that you received the updated school dress code. It's standard every year."

Dad signs with a big flourish, no questions asked, just like I knew he would. Then he looks at us both. "All righty then! I should get going so I don't hit weekend traffic. I'll miss you two!" He stands up and gives us both hugs.

I don't feel at all guilty about lying to him. As he likes to say, *You snooze, you lose.*

We follow Dad into the living room and watch as he packs his bag and folds up the faded floral guest bedding on the couch. Then he calls Aunt Nora to confirm she's picking up Mom. He probably knows he can only completely blow things once within the same week or we'll never forgive him.

I hover near our home phone, waiting for the robocall I know is coming. The school always calls if you're marked absent. As soon as it rings, I press one for excused absence and hang up. We'll deal with the parental permission note later.

"Was that your mother calling?" Dad asks when I come back into the room.

"What? No—another telemarketer. So annoying!" I say. "We get so many of those calls."

Dad nods and pats his shirt pocket. "That's why I only have my cell phone now. No one uses a landline."

He has his bag packed and shoes on, all before ten. "Guys, I loved seeing you both." He gives us each a kiss on our heads. "Even if it was for crappy reasons."

"Thanks for coming, Dad," I say, giving him a hug. He feels strong and warm underneath his old V-neck sweater.

"Yeah," Chance says. "Thanks."

"Next time we'll hang out in Philadelphia. Soon, I promise."

"Sure, Dad," I reply.

He slings his backpack over his shoulder and opens the front door. Chance and I follow him and stand on the front steps, waving goodbye to him as he pulls away in his old white Toyota Corolla.

As soon as his car disappears from view, Chance and I grab our bikes and pedal down to the center of town, straight to Joe's Barbershop.

"Ready?" Chance says, as we lock up our bikes out front.

"Ready as I'll ever be." I square my shoulders and push the glass door open, a bell jangling our arrival.

* * *

Two and a half hours later, we leave through the same ringing bell, my hair having magically morphed from my regular brown first to a bleached-out white-blond and then to its final color, Flamingo Pink.

"Whoa," Chance says for the hundredth time.

"Stop saying that!" I yell. "You're freaking me out!"

"Jose, it's so pink. I can't believe you went through with it. I was sure you'd wuss out before they even got to the bleaching, let alone the coloring."

"Thanks a lot," I say sarcastically.

"I mean, no offense. But seriously, I never thought you'd go through with it."

"Well maybe I'm not as boring as you think," I say. "I'm starving. That took forever."

"We're not going to school today, right?" Chance says, still staring at my head. "I mean, we've missed more than half of the day already."

"Definitely not!" I reply, giddy from adrenaline and hunger and knowing Mom is coming home today. Or maybe it's just the fumes from the hair color.

"Here, let's take a picture." Chance grabs my arm and holds his cell phone up high in front of our faces. "Say 'pink'!" We both break out in matching grins.

Just then a mother and her young son walk by holding hands. "Look, Mom!" he says loudly. "CLOWNS!"

The mother shushes him, and they keep walking. Chance and I share a glance and burst out laughing. For once I don't feel quite so embarrassed to stand out.

"What do you want to eat?" I ask Chance.

"What?" he asks, putting a hand behind his ear.

"I said, 'What do you want to eat?'" I repeat, louder this time.

"I can't hear you, the volume of your hair is deafening me." Chance laughs and juts his chin toward the retreating back of the little boy. "He's right, you know. All we need are red noses and some giant shoes and we could be in the circus."

I punch him on the arm. "Please stop, you're making me feel like a freak."

"Well, that's the point, right? To look a little freaky?"

"No, the point was to make a point about . . . oh, forget it!" I throw up my hands.

"Jose, I know you did this for me, and . . . I . . . um . . . thank you." Chance looks down shyly, all serious for once.

"I didn't just do it for you. I did it for Mom too."

I realize I'm making a dye job sound like I slayed a dragon or something equally heroic, but I hope when Mom gets back home, she'll take one look at me and see that I'm trying to be on Chance's side. And her side too.

But most of all, I did this for me. To do something brave.

"Come on, Pete's Diner is calling," Chance says, not noticing as a truck driver does a double, then triple take at us as we walk down the block, pushing our bikes along the sidewalk.

It hits me then that I'll probably be getting nonstop funny looks from now on. I didn't really consider that when I hatched my brilliant plan.

But there's not much I can do about it now. So I square my shoulders and look over to my brother, reassured by the sight of his now-familiar, bright-pink head bobbing along next to me.

22

After we pay the waiter, who teased me and Chance all through lunch, we take our bikes and ride home. Aunt Nora's minivan is already out front when we arrive.

We race inside.

"Mom?" I call out. "Aunt Nora?"

"In here," Aunt Nora's voice echoes from Mom's room.

Mom is sitting on her bed, leaning back against a huge beige pillow I've never seen before. It has arms on both sides and looks like it's giving her a hug. She's wearing a pair of black yoga pants and a black hoodie that's only halfway zipped up, and I can see white bandages underneath. Aunt Nora has her back to us and is unpacking things from Mom's suitcase.

"You're home!" I yell.

"Your hair!" Mom yells back, looking shocked. "Oh no! You too? It must be contagious."

I reach up self-consciously and tuck a strand of hair behind my ear. I thought it was weird at first when Chance kept forgetting why I was staring at him, but now I've forgotten about my hair too.

"Yeah, Mom, about that . . ." I start.

"Let's have a hug first," Mom says, reaching out one arm slowly. "Then you can tell me about it. Be gentle."

Chance and I hug Mom cautiously, away from her bandaged side. Then we sit down at the foot of her bed.

"So I dyed my hair," I start.

"Oh, really?" Aunt Nora says, with her usual cheerful voice. "I hadn't even noticed. I thought you'd been out in the sun, and it brought out your natural highlights."

"Ha ha, very funny, Aunt Nora."

"Is this going to be a problem at school?" Mom asks.

I look at Chance. He looks at me.

"Forget it," Mom says, shaking her head. "Right now, I don't want to know."

"You're not mad?" I ask. "I thought you might not like it."

Mom smiles. "Like it? I love it! I almost want to get mine done, but I don't think it would go over well at work."

"I like it too," Aunt Nora says. "Although I'm too old to do anything that crazy to my hair."

My cell phone beeps. I look down to see a message from Makayla. She must be texting during lunch period.

r u sick??? where are u today? you better be at the party tomorrow!!!

"Who's that?" Mom asks.

"Makayla," I say. "It's nothing."

"Is it about Autumn's party?" Chance asks.

"No," I say, quickly shoving my phone back into my pocket.

"What party?" Mom asks.

"Forget it," I say, hoping Chance will get the hint to drop it.

He doesn't.

"Autumn's having a party tomorrow night," he says. "Jose and I are invited."

"Oh," Mom says. "Tomorrow?"

"We don't have to go, Mom," I hurriedly add. "It's not a big deal."

Chance laughs. "What are you talking about? You and Makayla and the rest of the girls have been talking about it at school for weeks."

"We have not!" I protest.

"Don't you want to go?" Mom asks me.

I shrug. "I'd rather be home with you."

Aunt Nora doesn't say anything, but she and Mom give each other a look. I feel awful. I don't want Mom to think for a second that going to a party is more important than her being home from the hospital.

Even though I really, really want to go to Autumn's.

"Actually I don't want to go," I lie, feeling like crying. "Really! It will probably be boring."

"I don't believe you," Mom says, smiling.

"Me neither," Aunt Nora adds.

"Will Autumn's parents be there?" Mom asks Chance.

He shrugs. "I think so."

Why is my brother so dumb? You're supposed to say yes to a question like that!

Mom looks at me.

"I'm positive her mother will be there. She's going to get all the girls manicures," I tell her.

"Manicures? What's Chance supposed to do while you do that?"

"I come later," Chance says.

"Are her parents throwing another all-grade party?" Mom shakes her head. "Hats off to them, but they're crazy."

"It's not everyone," Chance says, not at all helpfully. "Just a few kids." He gets up off Mom's bed and stretches. "I'll be right back."

"Where are you going?" I ask. I can't believe he's leaving me to explain this party by myself.

"I have to use the bathroom!" he yells back. "Do you mind?"

Aunt Nora raises her eyebrows at Chance's retreating back, then turns to me. "So what you're not saying is that it's a boy-girl party?"

I'm getting annoyed with all their questions. "It's not a big deal," I say.

"Calm down," Mom says. "If there's an adult there for the entire time, you can go."

"Mom, are you sure?" I say. "You'll be home all alone."

"Hey!" Aunt Nora protests, giving me a friendly nudge. "What am I? Chopped liver?"

"Nora and I will be fine. You and Chance do your thing. I'm glad you have a party to go to." Then I notice that Mom is nearly crying.

"Mom? What's wrong?" I ask. "Are you OK?"

"Tissue," she gestures to her drippy nose. Aunt Nora hands her a box, laying on the bed alongside Mom and giving her hand a squeeze.

"I'm sorry, Josephine," Mom says. "Everything is OK."

I don't know what to say. I hate seeing Mom upset.

"If that's true, why are you crying?" I ask, confused.

"It's just everything," Mom says. "I'm so glad to be home. I think I was more nervous about being in the hospital than I realized. Now that it's over and I'm back home, I'm so relieved. Seeing you and Chance is the best part."

"We all need a good cry now and then," Aunt Nora says. "Your mom deserves it more than anyone. Here . . ." She pats the bed in between her and Mom. "Come sit down with us."

"Are you sure? I don't want to hurt you," I say.

"I'm sure, sweetheart. Come on. Don't worry." Mom blows her nose.

I lie down next to Mom.

"Allison, I'll go get you something to drink," Aunt Nora says, sitting up and kicking her legs over her side of the bed.

I sit up too.

"You stay," Aunt Nora says to me. "I'll do it."

A moment later, Mom's bedroom door clicks quietly shut. I close my eyes and feel her warmth next to me. She reaches over and pats me on the knee. "I love you," she says.

"Me too."

I feel like I've been right in this spot, with Mom, forever. It's so comforting.

"So Autumn's having another blowout?" Mom says. I can tell she's remembering the water park party and the Olympic athlete one. They are hard to forget.

"Yep," I reply. "I think it was supposed to be low-key." I giggle. "But Autumn's never had a low-key party in her life."

"Who else is coming?" Mom asks.

"Makayla," I say.

"Um-huh."

"And Anna and Emily."

"Right."

"And Chance."

"I didn't know Chance and Autumn were such good friends," Mom says, fishing for info.

"Yep, they're friends. Diego's coming too," I add in a rush. Then I look at her.

"Why do you look so suspicious?" Mom asks.

"It's the kind of party where we each invited one person who was a boy," I say quietly. I don't want to shock her, but I really want her to know about Diego. I'm so over having all these secrets in my life. What's the point? Besides, Mom likes Diego!

"OK . . ."

"And I thought it would be cool if Diego came." I blush. "He's the one I asked. I mean, Autumn asked him for me, but still."

"Are you going on a date?" She gasps.

"MOM! Of course not. We're just hanging out at a party. With adults there."

"So it's not a date?" she says.

"It's not a date," I insist.

"I can't believe you're going on a date!" Mom says, a big grin on her face.

"MOM! QUIT IT! You're not listening. It's. Not. A. Date."

"Fine, but whether it's a date or not, if there are no grown-ups there, you're coming right back home immediately. Got it?"

"OK," I say. I actually don't want to go to a boy-girl date party without a grown-up in the house, even though I'd never admit that to *anyone* in a billion years.

As I lie in bed next to Mom, her playing with the ends of my pink hair, I have this funny feeling that I've gotten superpowers. I'm not sure what they are or where they came from, but for the first time in my life, I feel like I'm a girl who could be named Magenta Clementine. She'd have a pet scorpion. And if there was something on her mind, she'd say it out loud, not keep it to herself.

Feeling brave, I take a selfie and send it to Makayla. About a second later my phone rings.

"AAAAAEEEEEEEEEEEEEEEEEEE!" Makayla screams in my ear so loud that even Mom jumps a bit.

"Shhh!" I say, leaving Mom's bedroom and shutting the door behind me. "You're going to break my eardrums."

"You look amazing!!!" Makayla shrieks. "When did you do that? I can't believe it. What happened to the tiny streak? Are you going to be in trouble with your mom?"

"No trouble," I say. "She got home from the hospital today. And she actually loves it."

"Ohmigod I'm so glad," Makayla says. "I bet you're so happy."

"I am soooo relieved!" I say. I take a deep breath. "But I feel weird about going to Autumn's party. My aunt is here keeping Mom company, but I don't know. It feels wrong going out when she's home stuck in bed."

"Did you ask your mom what she thinks?" Makayla says.

"She said Chance and I could go, but I still feel guilty." Then I start to cry. I can't tell if it's because Mom is home or because I feel guilty for wanting to go to the party anyway.

Makayla is silent as I sniffle into the phone. Then finally she says, "I think you should come to the party. Maybe it will cheer you up, you know? Especially if your mom is cool with it."

I sniffle more. "Yeah, maybe. I want to," I admit.

"Let me ask my mom if she can drive us both over to Autumn's tomorrow. That way we can go together! I'll text you after I ask her, OK?"

"OK," I say, feeling better. Still guilty, but better. "Thank you. I know I've been acting weird lately. Everyone must think I'm crazy."

"You haven't been weird. I mean, you have, but I totally get why! I'm glad. I mean, not glad at all about your mom," she rushes to add. "But I'm glad to know you're not mad at me!"

"Of course I'm not, Makayla. I thought you were mad at me."

"About what?" She sounds genuinely confused.

"I don't know. I guess it just seemed like you didn't care if I didn't go to Spirit Night."

"Jo, what are you talking about? I invited you to come, and you acted like you didn't want to. What did you expect me to do?"

All I can say back is, "Oh." She has a point.

Makayla keeps talking. "I'm not mad, but I wish you'd talk to me more. I feel like I'm always saying stuff to you, and you don't say anything important back."

"Like what?"

She starts rattling things off: "Like your dad or the divorce."

"We were eight!" I interrupt. "All we ever talked about was our American Girl dolls."

"Or when you like a boy. Or about your mom getting CANCER," she rushes on. "Most people complain about the smallest, stupidest things. It's OK to complain about the stuff that really sucks. Especially to me!"

"I know," I say, biting my cuticles. "It's just . . . sometimes I feel like talking about things makes them worse."

"That makes no sense." Makayla sounds surprised.

"It's how I feel. I hate talking! It makes me all churny. But I'm sorry about *us*. You're my favorite person ever."

"Same! I mean, not that *I'm* my favorite person ever. That you're my favorite person ever."

I giggle through my tears. "I know what you meant."

"I get that you're not super into oversharing, but please don't keep everything a secret from me. It makes me feel like we're not all that tight."

"What? That's not why I don't talk about things. You're my best friend."

"Best friends can tell each other anything," Makayla says. "No matter what. So will you please let me know next time something's up?"

I nod, even though she can't see me. "I promise."

"Jose," Chance says, walking into my room without knocking and handing me his cell phone. "It's for you."

"Hello?" I say into Chance's phone.

"No, it's a text for you, idiot." Chance takes the phone back and points to the screen. It's from Diego:

Chance sent me the photo of you two. You're as crazy as your brother!

I smile and text back: **LOL**

grandma would kill me if i did that to my hair. she'd say pink hair on a Mexican is no bueno, but it's awesome that you did it.

I smile. Then I send him a smiley face to show that I'm smiling.

I think it looks good! he writes back right away

TY!

YW!

I hear Makayla calling my name through my phone, but I ignore her.

Are you still coming tomorrow night to the party? Diego writes.

i think so

cool!

I blush.

"Whoa!" Chance says, reading over my shoulder. I jerk the phone away.

"Get away, Chance!" I scream at him.

"That's my phone, Jose," he says, grabbing it back. "I'll give Diego your number, I don't need your dumb texts to him clogging up my inbox."

I put my phone back to my ear and whisper to Makayla: "Diego likes my hair!!!"

"I told you it looks so cute! By the way, I already talked to my mom, and she said she can come tomorrow to pick you up, OK?"

"Thank you. I'm glad we're going together. I'd want to do that anyway."

We hang up. Then, still grinning, I text her: **xoxoxoox**

Xoxoxoxoo she writes back.

23

I spend Saturday morning trying on clothes for Autumn's party, attempting to figure out what goes with my newly pink hair. Bright colors are out—like my cute yellow hoodie—because they make me look like one of the My Little Ponies. By the time I finally settle on jeans and a black cut-out tee, there's a big mound of discarded clothing on my desk chair. On her way out the door to drive Chance to soccer practice, Aunt Nora reminds me to pack a sweater "just in case," so I toss a gray Westchester North Middle School sweatshirt into my backpack.

It's a beautiful, sunny fall day. The air smells amazing. My mom is back home and seems to be feeling OK. I'm invited to what Makayla won't stop calling "the party of the year." But that doesn't stop me from being sooo nervous!

I keep pacing around, going into the kitchen to open the fridge, not finding anything I like, and then walking back into my room. I even try to do homework—*ha*!

Finally I go into Mom's room to ask her if I can borrow a necklace but really, so I can be with her. She's in bed, laptop open, half watching a cooking show. Her eyes are sleepy-looking.

"Mom?"

She turns to me and smiles. "Hi, Josephine."

I sit down next to her on the bed to see what she's watching. I'm not surprised that it's *The Great British Baking Show*. She got into it over the summer and is now streaming the third season. Mom is a huge fan of Mary Berry.

She pauses the show. "Are you excited about today?"

I shrug. "Maybe I should stay home."

"Because of me?"

I shrug again. Partly I want to be with her, but mostly I'm anxious. I am so not ready to be part of a real, actual couple, and it seems like all the other girls going are. I don't want to tell her the mostly reason.

"It will be fun!" Mom insists. "Autumn is nice, right? And Makayla will be there."

I shrug again, harder.

"Nora will be here with me. I want you to go have fun. I'll probably nap."

"Why are you so tired?" I ask. I can't remember her ever napping.

She pats my knee. "I'm not so tired. I just feel like taking it easy."

"Because you're sick?"

Mom shakes her head. "Listen to me. I spoke to Dr. Chernoff yesterday. She said that if breast cancer is caught early, like mine was, it has a ninety-nine percent survival rate." She looks at me to make sure I'm listening. "We'll know more when my results come back. But even if it isn't caught early, breast cancer patients can live a long time. Something like ninety percent of patients are doing just fine at the five-year mark."

"Really?" I shift closer to Mom, smiling now.

"Yes, really. Dr. Chernoff said that's why she went into this particular field, because there's so much she can do to help. She's the one who told me that no one wants cancer, but if you have to have it, this is the one you want, remember?"

"So that means you're going to be OK? For real OK?"

Mom nods. "I'll need chemotherapy, which will make me feel really tired and really crappy for a while. It sounds awful. And honestly, I'm a little scared of what it will feel like. I'll probably lose my hair too. No one is pretending any of that will be fun for me, but treatment ends. And once it's over, I plan to go on living my life." Mom's eyes fill with tears. "My doctor promised me she'd fight to make sure that I'll be watching you and Chance graduate from college someday. She said she wants me to be able to dance at your weddings. I'll be here for all of it."

I lay my head on Mom's shoulder, and we sit there quietly for a few minutes, letting the happy sink in. I'm so relieved that I almost don't believe it. I can't wait to tell Chance.

After a few minutes of silence, Moms starts her baking show back up again, and before too long, she's asleep, breathing evenly. I take a minute to text Chance the good news. He replies with about a hundred thumbs-up emojis.

Eventually I tiptoe out of Mom's bedroom as quietly as possible and get myself a bowl of cereal. I sit in the kitchen until Chance and Nora arrive back from the soccer practice, carrying a pizza. Chance eats, like, two-thirds of the entire pie.

Makayla and her mom arrive at one in the afternoon to drive us to the girls-only half of the party.

Here we go, I think to myself, looking back over my shoulder as we pull away from my house. I wave, even though Aunt Nora already shut our front door and went back inside.

Once we're moving, Makayla tugs gently on a lock of my hair. "Your hair looks awesome," she says. "It's even pinker in person."

I giggle. "It is the pinkest."

"I can't get over it. You look so different. Right, Mom?"

Makayla's mom glances at me in the rearview mirror. "Completely different. I love it, Josephine."

"Thank you." Mrs. Kaiser has good taste, so I'm excited she likes it too. "I keep forgetting and then I look in the mirror and surprise myself."

They both laugh, like I'm making a joke, but I'm not.

We pull up to Autumn's parents' house, which is as amazing as ever, starting with the fancy gate that blocks our entrance until Mrs. Kaiser gives her name in the intercom. Only then do the massive doors swing open, slowly and dramatically. We drive up what's less like a driveway and more like a country road lined with trees. The leaves are just starting to change colors and hang over the car as we drive. The whole scene is like a greeting card.

About halfway up the drive, we pass a small house on the left.

"That's the groundskeeper's house," Makayla tells her mom. Mrs. Kaiser shakes her head but doesn't say anything.

We pull up to the front circular driveway, paved in stone, and come to a stop. Autumn comes running out of the house with a big smile on her face as we're climbing out of the car.

"YOUR HAIR LOOKS SO GOOD!" she screams, touching my head. "I LOVE IT!"

"Thanks," I say, ducking my head shyly.

"Hi, girls," says Autumn's mom, coming to the front door wearing super high heels, regular jeans, and a white T-shirt.

"Hi, Ms. Moore," Makayla says.

Autumn points at me. "Mom, this is Josephine. Josephine, that's my mom."

Ms. Moore smiles at me. "Of course I remember Josephine."

Ms. Moore used to be an actress on a soap opera. Autumn's dad was on the same show, playing her brother, but in real life they fell in love and got married. Now Autumn's dad is on another show, playing a spy with a sense of humor. Autumn's mom doesn't say anything about my hair. She doesn't even give it a second look. Probably all her training as an actress.

Autumn's mom goes to speak with Makayla's mom, and I guess whatever they talk about makes things seem OK as far as adult supervision, because Mrs. Kaiser leaves with a simple, "Have fun!"

"Girls, our chef is making sushi for lunch," Autumn's mom says as we head inside. "Did you bring your bathing suits?"

Makayla and I look at each other.

"Um, no," I say. I didn't realize we were going swimming. It's way too cold out.

"I did!" Makayla says. "I'm sorry, Josephine, I totally forgot to remind you to bring yours. Your hair distracted me."

"That's OK, I have a bunch. You can borrow one of mine," Autumn says. "Come on, Emily and Anna are already upstairs. Let's go!"

We go upstairs, and Emily and Anna greet us with hugs and tons of compliments about my hair. I'm feeling better about it by the second. Autumn's bedroom is massive. All her furniture and bedding are white, and her walls are white with pretty gold decorations like swirls and dots. There's a sheer white canopy over her bed and a white-and-gold rug.

Everything is perfect. Mom always says everyone has their problems, but right now it's hard to imagine Autumn having any at all. For a moment I feel a pang of jealousy. It's impossible not to think about how my own dinky room would fit into one tiny corner of Autumn's palatial space, or compare how we left Mom looking tired in bed while Autumn's mom zips around on high heels with a ton of energy.

But then I remember that:

1. Mom is home.

2. Aunt Nora is there with her.

3. Chance and I are getting along again.

4. And my hair is cute!

The main thing I feel is grateful and relieved. And even ready to have fun—finally!

Autumn opens her massive dresser drawer and motions for me to choose a bathing suit. I pick one with a blue and white tie-dye pattern on it—hoping it won't clash with my hair—and I go into her bathroom to get changed. Before we head down to the pool, I send Chance a quick text to make sure he knows to tell all the boys to bring bathing suits.

"Who are you texting?" Autumn asks, peeking over my shoulder. "Oooh! Chance. Tell him I said hi."

I obediently text him. He replies right away: *Tell her hi back.*

Autumn squeals reading the text, which makes everyone else ask what's going on. I tell them, and almost immediately everyone is shrieking and teasing Autumn. She's blushing, but she's laughing too.

I hope no one teases me about Diego. I can't handle it as gracefully as Autumn.

Once the excitement over Chance's text dies down, we head out to the pool. I worried about it being too cold to swim, but I should have known that Autumn's pool would be heated. Even though the air is cool, it doesn't matter. The water feels perfect. And there are heat lamps around the edges of the patio, so the air feels warm when we get out. It's just like swimming in the middle of summer.

After we swim, we wrap ourselves in fluffy white towels and eat. I've only had sushi twice before and don't like fish even when it's cooked, so I stick to veggie rolls with cucumber and sweet potato and stuff. Then we get our nails done by a manicurist named Deedee who brought tons of bottles of awesome colors. I can tell they're fancy, because instead of a label there's a tiny four-leaf-clover on the top of the bottle and nothing else. Deedee even lets us keep the color we pick for our nails.

Autumn explains that she decided against having someone come dye our hair because it would have taken too long but suggests we all go to Joe's some other time. "Mom was going to hire a makeup artist for us, though," she adds as our nails dry. "But I convinced her it was a little much."

I laugh, blowing on my electric blue nails. "Maybe just a little."

"Also," Emily adds, "makeup washes off in the pool."

"True." Autumn nods. "My mom says they never had any scenes on her soap where she got wet, because it was too much work to reapply makeup after a take."

"It would be funny if the boys showed up and we all had mascara dripping down our faces," Makayla says.

"If by *funny* you mean embarrassing!" Anna looks horrified.

The reminder that the boys are coming jolts me out of my mani-sushi-pool daze. In just a few hours I'll have to stand around in a bathing suit in front of all of them, including Diego. Suddenly my tie-dye bathing suit and blue nails and pink hair don't seem cute. I wish I could come up with a reasonable excuse to hide under a towel the whole time.

As the day goes on, everyone else is still talking nonstop, but the impending arrival of the boys has me worried. Without even realizing it, I get quieter and quieter. By the time we get changed back into dry clothing and head to the kitchen for some snacks, I'm almost mute.

"What's up with you?" Makayla finally whispers to me as I slink even lower into my chair. "You're so quiet."

I think about saying, *Nothing*, but then I remember my promise not to keep everything a secret. So instead I blurt out, loud enough for all the other girls to hear, "What if all the boys think I look like a freak? I don't even know how to kiss because I've never done it before."

Everyone stops and gawks at me. I feel my face getting red.

"What? No way! You look like a rock star," Autumn says. "I love your hair. And kissing isn't that hard. You just move your lips around like this." She makes a face like she's trying to get peanut butter out of her teeth.

I crack up. "Thanks, I'll do that."

"I love your hair too," Emily says. "I am so jealous! My mom would *die* if I did that." She looks embarrassed. "I mean, not like anything about your mom, Josephine."

"I know that's not what you meant," I say, cringing a little inside just hearing the word *mom*.

"I love it too," Makayla says. "And you love it, right?"

I shrug. Then I smile. "I love it, even though I look like a clown."

"Then who cares what anyone else thinks? And you don't look like a clown! You look so pretty."

"And . . . now that you mention it . . . I've actually never kissed anyone else, either," Anna says, giving me a sympathetic look.

Everyone looks at her. Instantly, I feel better.

"Really?" I say.

She shakes her head. "Never. So everyone else has?"

Emily and Autumn nod.

"At my nature camp," Emily says.

"On vacation last Christmas," Autumn chimes in.

"At Spirit Night, with Noah," Makayla says, looking a little embarrassed.

We all sit silently for several seconds, then everyone—even me—lets out a collective shriek at top volume.

"HOW COULD YOU HAVE KEPT THAT A SECRET FROM ME?" I yell, laughing at her. I'm not mad, but I am a little glad to bust her for not telling me something instead of the other way around for once.

"It was just for a second," Makayla says. "It was a goodbye kiss. It hardly counts."

Everyone shrieks again.

"Cut it out!" Makayla says. "I wanted to tell you guys, but I was worried that he would stop liking me before the party and then it would be even worse with everyone knowing he was my first kiss."

"What?" Emily says. "Why would he stop liking you?"

I'm surprised at that too. Makayla is always so confident about Noah. Or at least she acts like it.

"It's hard to know what boys are thinking," Makayla says. "I can't tell for sure."

"He'd be the biggest idiot if he didn't like you," I say. "Because you're the greatest."

Everyone says, "Awwww," and Makayla hugs me.

I don't mind at all.

Eventually we run out of things to do and talk about, so we decide to watch a movie. Or pretend to watch a movie, at least. No one is really paying attention, because we're all on our phones. Things get increasingly silent as it gets closer to six o'clock, and finally Autumn clicks off the TV, even though the movie isn't over.

Maybe I'm not the only one nervous about the boys coming over.

I hope Chance and Aunt Nora will show up on time. Chance is always good at making things less awkward.

At 6:01 I text him: **Are u on yr way? HURRY UP!**

Almost there. Just have to get up the driveway. That should take another 20 mins or so. LOL.

"Chance is almost here," I say to Autumn, showing her the text. She jumps up, and everyone starts screaming and running around.

"It's just Chance!" I yell after their retreating backs, following them back through the house and to the front door.

A moment later, the doorbell rings, and Chance walks in with Diego, both carrying backpacks. Diego is wearing shorts and flip-flops, which is kind of crazy considering October in Westchester isn't all that warm, but one year he wore shorts every day up until Thanksgiving break, so he must not get cold legs.

I wave shyly, ducking my head. Diego waves back.

"Happy birthday!" Chance says, giving Autumn a hug that lifts her off the ground. She giggles.

"Chance, is Aunt Nora here?" I ask.

"She's outside talking to Autumn's mom," he says.

I want to ask how Mom is, but I don't want to do it in front of everyone. Then the doorbell rings again, and Noah, Ryan, and Jacob are piling in, and the house is filled with noise.

"Autumn, let's swim!" Anna says, clapping her hands. "It's so nice in the pool."

"Sure," Autumn says.

"Where should I change into my bathing suit?" Diego looks around in confusion. "How big is this house?"

Autumn laughs. "Come on, I'll show you where the pool house is. The boys can change in there, and the girls can use the downstairs guest bathrooms."

"There's more than one downstairs guest bathroom?" I whisper to Emily. She nods back, all NBD.

Our house doesn't have any guest bathrooms, let alone a pool house, and in Dad's apartment the bathroom doesn't even have a sink. After you use the toilet, you have to come out and wash your hands in the kitchen sink. Dad says it's old-fashioned, but it's not. It's just weird.

I hate putting on a wet bathing suit—it's such a gross feeling—but we all get changed again, and then we swim, eat pizza, swim more, and do cannonballs.

I know that makes it sound really adorable, like a five-way double date or something, but for most of the evening, the boys basically ignore the girls and vice versa. It's just like going to the town pool during the summer—if the town pool had sparkling white towels that smelled awesome instead of all chorine-y and offered unlimited free snacks and wasn't full of little kids crying about not wanting to take swim lessons.

While we're in the pool, Autumn's mom has some guy come set up the firepit so we can make s'mores. Still wearing our bathing suits, we all cluster around with metal sticks full of marshmallows. I wrap myself in a towel, careful not to let it get near the flames. The last thing I need is to light my towel on fire and have to stand in front of all the boys half-dressed!

Up until then, I haven't said more than ten words to Diego, five of which are, "Could you pass the Doritos?" I tried to smile at him a couple times, and he gave me kind of a friendly-ish nod, but that's it.

I'm standing next to Emily, roasting my marshmallow, when I hear her whispering with Makayla about something.

"If it's empty, it will spin too many times," Makayla says.

"What about half full?"

I lean toward them and whisper, "What are you two talking about?"

Emily, who's on Makayla's other side, answers in a loud voice: "Spin the bottle. We need a water bottle that's half full. Who's in?"

Everyone gets awkwardly quiet. No one says anything.

"Here's a bottle!" Makayla says, grabbing an empty water bottle from a nearby table. She dunks it in the pool to fill it halfway.

Emily gestures for us to follow her, and we all put our sticks down by the side of the firepit and race into the pool house, trying not to call attention to ourselves. Looks like spin the bottle is happening, whether I want it to or not.

Emily grabs the bottle from Makayla. "Autumn, it's your birthday. You go first!"

Autumn takes the bottle, not looking in Chance's direction. After all our talk of kissing earlier and it's only now that I wonder if Chance has kissed anyone. *Who would he have kissed? And when?*

But Autumn's mom must be watching us like a hawk from inside, because she comes to check on us at the exact moment Autumn puts the bottle down on the ground. She pretends she's there to see if we need more marshmallows, but I'm pretty sure she knows what Emily and Makayla were planning.

"Whew," I mutter under my breath so no one else hears. I am not ready for kissing anyone yet.

We go back outside to eat our abandoned marshmallows and s'mores, which are so messy that we all have to jump back into the pool to de-goop our fingers and mouths. Between Autumn's mom coming in and out to offer us more soda and water—but really to keep an eye on us—and the firepit guy supervising so we don't catch ourselves on fire, it's totally not the party I expected it to be.

Less wild. More regular.

As the first parents arrive, we all start hugging good night. I mean all the boys hug all the girls, then the girls hug each other, then the boys all awkwardly arm-pat one another in a jokey way.

While we're waiting for Aunt Nora, Chance stands next to Autumn and shows her something on his phone while I hover nearby with nothing to do. That's when Diego finally comes up to talk to me. He's still in his black bathing suit, with a gray T-shirt on top. His normally spiky hair is lying flat and in a center part. It looks funny. He's still cute, although maybe not as cute as usual.

"Hey," he says. He gestures to our surroundings. "Cool house, right?"

I nod, feeling shy.

He motions to my hair, which I've got in a bun on top of my head, and then to my brother. "How do you like being an identical twin with that guy?"

I laugh. Diego is right. We do look like twins—for real—for the first time ever. "It's not so bad," I say.

"I like it." He smiles at me, and I smile back. "It looks better on you than on him."

"Thanks."

"So . . . do you ever go to the movies?" Diego asks, shuffling his feet like he's nervous.

I shrug. "Sometimes." My heart is beating super fast now.

"Maybe you'll come with me next weekend? I mean, if your mom feels OK? To see a movie?"

Is this him asking me out? I wish I could freeze everything for a second and text Makayla to ask her opinion, but it's just Diego and me, and I have to answer him.

"I'd like that," I say. "I mean, I'd like to see a movie. With you."

Diego smiles a big smile at me and pushes his hair back with his hand. It stands up a little, and he looks as cute as ever. Then Autumn's mom calls, "Diego, your dad is here!" and Diego looks both relieved and disappointed at once.

Just like me.

We give each other a quick, stiff hug, and that's it. He's gone, and my heart settles back down to regular old beating.

When Aunt Nora arrives, only a minute or two later, to pick Chance and me up, I realize that after all the hype, there will be no kissing or sitting next to each other holding hands or anything after all. After all that worrying!

"How's Mom?" Chance asks Aunt Nora the second we're settled into the car and making our way down the winding path.

"She took a nap this afternoon and has mostly been resting, but she said she's feeling better than she expected," Aunt Nora answers.

"Did she miss us?" I hope she didn't.

Aunt Nora shakes her head with a smile. "Nope! You weren't gone all that long. Besides, I kept her busy watching episodes of *The Bachelorette* all afternoon. Your mom got to hear me scream at the television."

We tiptoe inside when we get home, not wanting to wake Mom up, but I can't help opening her bedroom door—just a crack—when I pass by. She's lying on her side under the covers, her back to me, completely still. For a second, I panic and think, *Is she breathing?* But then I see her move slightly, and my thundering heart starts to slow.

Aunt Nora comes up behind me and pats me on the shoulder. "Your mother is going to be fine," she whispers.

"I know," I say. I turn away, not wanting to watch Mom sleep anymore. It feels wrong and a little scary. "Good night, Aunt Nora."

"Good night, sweetie. Sleep well."

I change into my nightgown and climb into bed, falling asleep after making two wishes:

1. That Diego was amazed by my awesomeness and charm at the party and shows up tomorrow with a dozen roses or, like, two gray doves.

2. That Mom will be feeling well enough in the morning to talk about the party and look through the cute new party swag bag that Autumn gave us.

* * *

One wish comes true: The next morning Mom is alert and excited to hear about the party. I tell her about the sushi, and the snacks, and Autumn's room, and I show her my fancy nails, and the new tote bag with my name monogrammed on the side, along with the fuzzy, white terry cloth bathing suit cover-up—also monogrammed— that Autumn gave each of the girls.

I walk around Mom's bedroom, pretending to be a model, with the cover-up on over my jeans and a sweat-shirt. There are no matching doves on the front porch from Diego, but I do get a bunch of texts from the other girls talking about how fun the party was, and Autumn sends all sorts of cute photos that her mom took of us get-ting ready before the boys came.

Which was totally the most fun part of the night.

I can't believe it! Why does everyone always make such a big deal about love? It's in every book, movie, and song. How come there aren't more songs about how awe-some it is to have friends? Talking to one another about who'd been kissed and who hadn't was my favorite part of the whole event.

That and the s'mores.

OK and maybe the last two minutes I got to spend one-on-one with Diego.

I keep smiling and showing Mom the pictures. "This is Emily," I say.

"Oh my goodness, I remember when you two were in kindergarten together!" Mom sighs. "You all look so grown up."

"Here's Makayla's and my hands. See, we got matching nail art."

Mom squints at my phone. "Very nice."

In a bunch of photos, my hair is wet from swimming, so it looks like I have a bright pink cap on.

"I missed you the whole time!" I say to Mom as she flips through my slideshow, not wanting her to think I forgot about her.

Even though, for a few hours, I did.

Maybe I didn't think about her nonstop for the whole evening, but everything is better now that she's home. Having her back where she's supposed to be is reassuring. I hope she won't have to go anywhere again for a long time.

Mom hugs me with her good side. "You don't need to miss me, honey. I'm right here."

24

You'd think after rocking pink hair, successfully surviving Autumn's birthday party without making an idiot of myself, *and* having Mom home, I'd feel invincible, but my newfound bravery is like a 24-hour stomach virus. It passes as quickly as it came on. By Sunday evening, after eating reheated lasagna with Mom and Aunt Nora, I can't stop worrying about how Mr. Malik will react to my hair, especially considering he sent home a whole thing about the dress code.

When Chance and I get on the bus Monday morning, I'm not feeling like a goddess of pink hair and bad attitude. I'm a total wreck.

Our bus driver does a double take as soon as we board. He just got used to Chance's head, and now here we are looking like the Pink Doublemint Twins.

"Hey, hey, hey!" Mr. Mike cheerfully shouts out as he slams the door shut behind us. "Lookie here. What's up, Pinkie?"

I blush and look down. Everyone is staring at me. Chance strides down the bus aisle, not noticing as his bag smacks along the seats. He hops over Oliver's legs and sits down by a window.

My taking a stand suddenly seems a whole lot less brilliant and a whole lot more stupid. We are going to be in some serious trouble with Principal Malik, I know it, even if Chance is acting like it's a regular old day.

I grab the seat next to Lucy Weinman, a shy sixth grader who always sits right behind Mr. Mike. Then I won't have to pass row after row of staring, curious faces.

"Be brave, Josephine," I whisper under my breath. "Be brave."

Lucy says something to me, but I can't hear it over the roar of the bus engine.

"What?" I say.

"I said, your hair is nice," Lucy repeats, louder this time.

"Thank you." I smile at her.

"I totally want to dye my hair too," she says.

"You should," I tell her. "You'd look good in green, maybe."

Lucy shakes her head. "I'm too worried I'll look dumb."

"Trust me, I am the biggest chicken in the world. There's nothing to worry about. You can always dye it back if you hate it."

Lucy pulls her dark blond hair in front of her eyes. "It makes you look older," she says, examining me closely. "Like you should be in a band, you know?"

"Really?" I'm delighted. No one has ever said anything like that about me before.

When our bus lets us off at school, I can feel the stares of people as I walk down the hallways. It's so uncomfortable. People are covering their mouths and turning to say stuff to their friends.

Are they all laughing at me?

I hear Chance's voice in my head, saying, *Josephine, so what? Who cares if they are?* So I square my shoulders and stand up tall, like tree-pose tall, my head reaching up to the sky. I force myself to look back at people instead of ducking and running for cover.

Chance and I turn a corner and are about to pass by Mr. Malik's office. My heart speeds up again. Mr. Malik likes to greet kids in the morning as they walk by his door. Why didn't I think of that sooner?

Sure enough, there he is. The principal is greeting a group of students ahead of us, but when he catches sight of me his smile drops. I can see his eyes narrowing as Chance and I get closer, then he gives us the look—the one teachers have been giving to Chance since he was in kindergarten.

I've never had anyone give me the You're-in-trouble look before. It's both terrifying and exciting.

"In my office, you two," Mr. Malik says, gesturing behind him with a jerk of his thumb. His voice is stern. "I'll be there in a minute. You can wait inside."

"OK," I mumble, trying to look appropriately chagrined.

"See?" Chance whispers to me as we take our seats in Mr. Malik's office. "I told you, nothing to worry about."

"What are you talking about? We're in trouble right now."

Chance gives me a friendly shove. "Trust me, this is nothing. If we were in real trouble he wouldn't have sent us in ahead of him. He'd have marched us in here himself."

A few endless minutes later, Mr. Malik comes in and sits down at his desk, sighing as he looks at both of us. "Perhaps you didn't read the booklet on our dress code?"

"What booklet?" Chance asks.

Mr. Malik turns to me.

"Josephine? Did you read it?"

I nod. "I read it, Mr. Malik."

"Then can I ask why your hair is dyed pink? It's . . . unacceptable."

I feel my face heat, and then I start crying. "Mr. Malik, I'm sorry, but it's for our mom. She has cancer!"

Mr. Malik taps his fingers against his desk and focuses on a spot over my shoulder. "I know, and I'm sorry." His voice is gentler now. "I don't think your mother wants you to get into trouble, though."

"Maybe not," I say, cutting Chance off before he can speak. "But it's our mom, and she needs our support. The pink hair is for her. Not for anyone else."

"So you don't mind going to detention today, then?"

I shrug, still crying a little bit. "It's worth it."

Mr. Malik sighs and stands up. "Why don't we discuss this later? You need to get to class. But you'll both need to resolve . . . that"—he points to my head—"and soon. I can't allow it at school. It's too distracting."

I start to reply, but Chance grabs me by my elbow and yells, "Thank you!" behind him as he pulls me out of the room.

"What just happened?" I ask him.

"You got us out of trouble by crying. Great work!"

"I didn't cry to get us out of trouble, you dolt."

Chance sighs. "I know you didn't, Jose. It's OK."

I walk with my brother down the hall. People stare. Some people whisper. But the skies don't open up, and the ground doesn't swallow me. I'm still standing, just like always, putting one Converse-clad foot in front of another, like it's any other day.

I glance over at Chance, who makes a goofy face back at me.

"Go, Jose!" He high-fives me. "Welcome to the dark side."

"No, thank you." I laugh. "No dark side for me."

"You gotta admit, it's not so bad, is it?"

I roll my eyes at him. There's nothing else to do with my brother.

We walk by the art room, and it makes me think about that awesome quote from Georgia O'Keeffe that Mr. Fabel has hanging up on his bulletin board: "I've been absolutely terrified every moment of my life—and I've never let it keep me from doing a single thing I wanted to do."

I never really understood that before. Why do something if you're totally terrified? But now I can see why. I'm not any less worried than I was before, but for once, I'm not letting that stop me. I still don't feel like I rule the school, but no one has died of shame. Chance was right. Again.

I wonder what's going to happen next. With Mom and Diego, not to mention with Mr. Malik and my hair. But I push all those thoughts out of my head, just for a minute. I deserve to enjoy my moment without freaking out about the future. Beaming, I walk to my next class, my heart full of happy feelings, letting myself enjoy every single one.

I come in late, and Mrs. Grunwald stops what she's doing to look at me with wide eyes. "Josephine, your hair."

"I know!" I say, my voice as bright as my hair. "I love it too."

Acknowledgments

Thank you to my Capstone editor, Alison Deering, whose edits, suggestions, and enthusiasm made every page of *Pink Hair and Other Terrible Ideas* stronger, and to the rest of the talented Capstone team, including Jennifer Glidden and Shannon Hoffmann.

Big thanks to my agent, Jennifer Laughran, for her support and savvy (and her excellent podcast, Literaticast, which I certainly never listen to when I should be writing). Nell and Emma, your notes and advice made writing this story infinitely more fun and less lonely, and I appreciate your making the time for our writing group.

Finally, I wish I didn't have first-hand knowledge of what it's like to have a parent with cancer, but I do. My mother taught me many things—not giving up without a fight was one of the most important. I only wish she were here to see how the story turned out.

About the Author

Andrea Pyros is the author *My Year of Epic Rock*, which was called "a perfect read for anyone who feels BFF-challenged" by *Booklist* and "a charming addition to upper elementary and middle school collections" by *School Library Journal*. Andrea is a contributor to the popular website From The Mixed-Up Files of Middle Grade Authors and has written extensively for young adults, starting with her stint as co-founder of the pop culture website Girls on Film and then as a senior-level editor at a variety of teen magazines.

A native of New York City, Andrea now lives in New York's Hudson Valley with her husband and their two children. For more information, visit her at www.andreapyros.com.